Blaine wanted Donovan

More than ever, she wanted to make love to him. Fiery, passionate love. The kind that burned away all petty worries. She stared at his profile, wondering how to approach him.

"It's getting awfully hot in here," she whispered.

He looked around the room for a thermostat. "Want me to turn down the—" He broke off, as if he suddenly realized she wasn't talking about the temperature. "Well...what do you want?"

Blaine shifted in her seat. Outside, the rush of rain and wind sounded like someone whispering, "Lovers."

Lovers. The thought thrilled her.

"What do I want?" To show him, she pressed her lips against his neck, taking tiny, nibbling bites. Emboldened by her fired-up libido and his sharp intake of breath, she leaned close to his ear and whispered, "I want to devour you."

Dear Reader,

A year ago, my editor visited me in Colorado. We took a day trip to Manitou Springs, a lovely town nestled in the foothills of Pikes Peak, and we were talking about my writing a WRONG BED book. At that moment we walked past an old antique store with the most beautiful, ornate brass bed in the window and my editor pointed at it and said, "There's your Wrong Bed story."

And that's the moment *Lightning Strikes* began taking shape in my mind. The story opens when Blaine Saunders, down on her luck and out taking a mind-cleansing stroll, is lulled into a store by a sensuously magical brass bed in the window. And on a whim, practical Blaine has a spontaneous moment and buys the bed!

That's just the beginning of more spontaneous moments in Blaine's life—moments filled with fun, sensuality and some steamy adventures with a dark, handsome stranger who falls into her life, and into that brass bed....

I invite you to visit my Web site, www.colleencollins.net, where you can read about my upcoming Temptation novels, enter contests and more.

Enjoy *Lightning Strikes!* And like the heroine in the story, do something fun and sensual for yourself on a whim....

Best wishes,

Colleen Collins

Books by Colleen Collins

HARLEQUIN TEMPTATION
867—JOYRIDE
899—TONGUE-TIED

HARLEQUIN DUETS
10—MARRIED AFTER
    BREAKFAST
22—ROUGH AND RUGGED
30—IN BED WITH THE PIRATE
39—SHE'S GOT MAIL!

LIGHTNING STRIKES
Colleen Collins

HARLEQUIN®

TORONTO • NEW YORK • LONDON
AMSTERDAM • PARIS • SYDNEY • HAMBURG
STOCKHOLM • ATHENS • TOKYO • MILAN • MADRID
PRAGUE • WARSAW • BUDAPEST • AUCKLAND

I'd like to dedicate this book to the Common Grounds coffee shop in Denver where I've sipped many lattes and written many romances. And thanks to my great friends in Denver with whom I shared lots of laughter and good times. John and Ralph, save a chair for me at the "Little Bear."

And thank you to my editor, Wanda Ottewell, for her ongoing encouragement and support.

ISBN 0-373-69113-0

LIGHTNING STRIKES

Visit us at www.eHarlequin.com

Printed in U.S.A.

1

BLAINE SAUNDERS GLIDED her fingers along the cylindrical metal and closed her hand tightly around it, loving its hard, smooth texture. Then she sucked in a gasp of air and sneezed.

Damn allergies. Still gripping the section of metal on the brass headboard, Blaine stuffed her other hand into her pants pocket and withdrew one of the always-present tissues she kept handy this time of year. Just a few minutes ago, she'd sneezed her head off outside the Spice of Life coffee shop, one of her fav haunts in Manitou Springs. But then, almost everywhere in Manitou was a fav haunt—what wasn't to like about a picturesque mountain community filled with quaint shops and winding streets nestled at the base of Colorado's Pikes Peak?

But when summer hit, the temperatures spiked and the afternoon thunderstorms rolled in, changing the cozy little town into a bowl of pollen.

She blew her nose. *June should be declared Pollen Month.*

Tucking away the tissue, Blaine brushed her fingers along the glistening headboard and imagined how pleasurable it would be to sleep in this beauty every single night. She leaned closer, catching her reflection in its polished surface. The shimmering metallic image gave her big green eyes and shoulder-length auburn hair a magical allure she never felt in everyday life. If she held her head a little higher, her gold-tinged reflection looked almost like Liv Tyler in *Lord of the Rings*.

Blaine sighed deeply. Then coughed. *Damn allergies.*

Dabbing the tissue at her nose, she stroked her finger in a lazy path along a metallic curve, enjoying the streak of moisture left from her hot skin making contact with the cool metal. So cool. So hot outside. *Would anyone notice if I pressed my hot face against this cool metal?*

She looked around. Jerome, the store owner, stood by a window, his hair glinting silver in a stream of sunlight, where he fastidiously dusted off an antique cabinet. But no one else was around. *Great.* She leaned over and pressed her forehead, then her cheek, against the sleek metal.

Ahhhhhh.

This had to be better than sticking her face in front of a fan, which she'd been doing back at her office all morning long. Especially after David called to announce he was engaged to another girl, although the fan didn't, unfortunately, blow away her disappointment. So she'd reminded herself that four months of Thursday-night dates didn't necessarily equate to ever-after.

For David, it didn't equate to exclusivity either, it appeared.

But for Blaine, it had been a close-enough, sorta-boyfriend situation that she'd suggested they take a romantic Alaskan cruise, a dream she'd nursed since grammar school when she'd written a report on the northern lights. When David agreed, Blaine had exuberantly spent her income tax return on a cruise ticket. Which she'd been on her way to get a cash refund for when this beguiling bed had snagged her attention.

She pressed her cheek harder against the metal, loving its sleek, cool texture. If only men were like this. Stable, reassuring, cool when it was hot outside...hot when it was cool inside...

"Blaine, dear, are you all right?"

Blaine, her cheek still pressed to the section of brass bed, shifted her gaze. Jerome stood stiffly next to her, his gray, cookie-duster mustache twitching. His gaze darted to the metal pressed to her cheek, then back to her eyes.

"I'm fine," she murmured, easing ever so casually to a standing position, hoping she didn't have a cylindrical indent on her cheek. Jerome's cologne, which always smelled like spicy orchids to her, traced the air.

"Still haven't fixed your air-conditioning?"

"When my accounts pay up, I might."

In the moment of silence that followed, Blaine knew that Jerome knew *exactly* what she was talking about. Several months ago, Jerome had hired Blaine to organize an estate sale, for which he had yet to pay. As owner of the Blaine Saunders Temporary Agency, she normally brokered temporary personnel for others— anything from accounting to technical writing—but because Jerome had been an old friend of her mother's, Blaine had taken on management of the estate sale herself.

Then, the economy took a surprising nosedive. Businesses started cutting back on everything from office supplies to employee head count. The latter hit Blaine's business hard because before a company reduced its own employee base, it eliminated all workers contracted through outside agencies. Which was, unfortunately exactly what the Blaine Saunders Temporary Agency specialized in—contracting workers, from secretaries to database specialists, to businesses.

Almost overnight, she lost three-fourths of her contracts with local corporations. To make ends meet, Blaine had moved out of her condo and rented a small room in someone's house. And she applied for a small-business loan, which she'd hear soon if the bank approved or not. She'd also requested her outstanding accounts to please pay up, but when Jerome had pleaded tight finances, she'd told him to pay when convenient.

Which made her feel a tad guilty for her quick retort, but if Jerome wanted to mention her not being able to fix things, well...

He glanced around his shop, then leaned forward slightly. "You're second on my list," he said under his breath. "Right after I pay Ralph."

"Ralph?" She thought she knew everyone in Manitou Springs.

"He delivers the antiques to my customers." Straightening, Jerome raised his voice. "Heard your father's working with you."

When the economy faltered, her dad had volunteered to help Blaine out at the agency. Having let go of her part-time assistant, Blaine had appreciated her dad's offer. Plus, she knew he welcomed a respite from spending the bulk of his retirement years parked in front of a TV.

"Yes, he's having a wonderful time playing receptionist," Blaine said. *And a wonderful time playing matchmaker, or trying to.* She had yet to tell him about David getting engaged to another woman...Blaine felt bad, yes, but she knew her father would be downright devastated.

A slightly crooked lamp shade caught Jerome's eye. "Also heard your sister's getting married." He reached for the shade and leveled it with a flick of his fingertips.

Sonja, Blaine's kid sister, had always been one for surprises. Her most recent being her news that she planned to elope in a week with a cadet who'd just graduated from the prestigious Air Force Academy in nearby Colorado Springs. Their dad, after darn near kissing the ground, had convinced Sonja to at least have a small ceremony in town, claiming it's what her dearly departed mother would have wanted.

"Yes, she's getting married," Blaine affirmed, realizing Jerome had successfully steered the conversation away from his debt. "Mom would have been so proud."

Ever since they had lost her to cancer fifteen years ago, Blaine had been a surrogate mom to Sonja. Which hadn't been bad because practical, tomboyish Blaine got to live out all the fun girly stuff through her popular sister Sonja.

Jerome's voice interrupted Blaine's thoughts. "It's a beautiful bed, isn't it?"

Blaine eyed the glistening brass beauty that had lured her into Jerome's shop. "It's gorgeous," she whispered, her fingers playing along one of the shiny cylinders that curled seductively in the headboard. She tried to imagine the bed in the cramped room she was renting, but realized there was no way this exquisite object could even begin to fit in the door, much less the room.

Jerome touched a veined hand to the brass knob that topped one of the four posters of the bed. "Just received it yesterday," he said, the pride evident in his voice. "We've already had an offer."

"An offer?" Blaine's fingers tightened possessively on a bend of metal.

"Yes." Jerome lifted the price tag, a square red label that dangled from a section of brass. "They said they'd return today, by noon. I'm hoping they want to at least make a down payment..."

By noon? She jerked her head to her wrist and checked the time. Eleven fifty-five. "They can't!" she blurted.

Jerome cocked one white eyebrow. "Blaine, I do believe the heat's gotten to you. You never raise your voice."

"When it's important, I do." And suddenly, this bed was very, very important.

"And what's so important about this bed?"

Because it symbolizes everything I'm not, and everything I've secretly desired—passion, fantasy, forbidden indul-

gences. "Because...it'd be a perfect wedding gift for Sonja." That sounded better than to admit she coveted it. But on second thought, she realized it *would* be perfect for Sonja and her husband-to-be.

"Is Sonja's betrothed going to buy it?"

Blaine pursed her lips. Hardly. Sonja's fiancé, Rudy, was on a squeaky-tight budget.

"No," she answered, tilting her head to see the price on that red tag. She blinked at the string of numbers, and comma. Two-thousand-plus dollars. Hoo-boy. Even though, after cashing in her cruise ticket, she'd have double that much, she didn't need to splurge half of it on a *bed*.

The slam of a car door distracted Blaine.

A pleased expression crossed Jerome's face as he peered out the plate glass window. "Ah, there they are now."

Blaine glanced out the window. A couple who looked to be in their forties were getting out of one of those ritzy sports cars. They looked supercoiffed, as though they never wrinkled or sweated. As they headed across the street toward the antique shop, Blaine wondered if they always sauntered as though they didn't have a care in the world. And more, what it felt like to not have any worries or cares.

The couple entered the shop, eyed Jerome, and waved a greeting. "We wanted to look at it one more time," the woman called out in a singsong voice.

Blaine tightened her grip.

The couple approached the bed, then walked slowly around it, inspecting it.

"It's a bit high," the woman murmured.

Thanks to the rose scent from the woman's perfume, Jerome's exotic-orchid scent and the world of pollen, it took all of Blaine's willpower to not explode a sneeze that could move this bed to the next county. She had to be alert, pay attention. The bed was at stake.

"The height has an advantage," commented Jerome, folding his hands neatly on top of each other. "You can store things underneath, saving room in the bedroom."

The woman arched one unnaturally blond eyebrow. "And the brass...the color isn't uniform."

"It's an antique," Jerome explained. "It's aged with time, like a fine wine."

The woman sighed and placed her hand on her husband's arm, her thin, tan wrist adorned with a sparkling tennis bracelet. "I'm not sure, darling. I want an antique, yes, but this looks so...so *old*..."

Jerome glanced at his wristwatch. "Well, I promised I'd hold it for you until noon, which is in two minutes..."

In the following silence, Blaine looked at the piece of magic before her. It was to die for. Ornate curves of brass that begged to be stroked and explored. A plump mattress that cried out for more than sleeping. Yes, this would be the ultimate wedding gift for Sonja, who had zilch furniture for her new life. And this way, Blaine could visit the bed, enjoy it vicariously as she'd always vicariously enjoyed other things in her sister's life.

But it was more than just a bed. Or living vicariously through her sister. Suddenly, with a surge of desperation and defiance, Blaine realized how tired she was of losing things. Losing a sorta-boyfriend, losing her condo, on the verge of losing her business. It was time for Blaine Saunders to win something, damn it! Something glorious, exotic, indulgent.

She had to win this bed!

Blaine cocked her head and scrutinized it. She cleared her throat. "This bed is *much* too high," she said in a low, blasé voice as though she often analyzed things like expensive brass luxuries. She slid a conspiratorial look at the couple. "Did you read about that incident at The Broadmoor recently?" She paused, letting the name of the nearby superexclusive hotel sink in. "Seems some old, high brass bed collapsed in the middle of the night. The wife survived...but..." Blaine made a tsking sound under her breath.

The woman glanced nervously at her husband. "Darling, can we talk for a moment?"

As the couple sauntered off, whispering, Jerome jerked his head toward Blaine. "What in God's name are you doing?"

"Trying to not implode in front of those nice people." When Jerome stared at her, she explained. "Allergies."

"I didn't know allergies turned people into storytellers." He gave his head a shake. "Collapsing beds. The Broadmoor."

She smiled sweetly. "Jerome, when are you paying Ralph?"

He shifted her a look. "I said you were second on my list—"

"I never put myself first, Jerome, but right now I

have the urge. Make me first." She batted her eyes with great exaggeration, which coaxed a smile from the older gentleman.

He lowered his voice. "Blaine, honey, you got your mama's eyes. And when you put your mind to it, her wicked charm, too."

Blaine grinned, remembering her mom's sassy, stubborn ways. Maybe Blaine didn't get Sonja's curly blond hair and ultrafeminine style, but she'd happily call it even if she got her mom's personality.

Jerome's smile faded. "But, unfortunately, I don't have the cash."

Blaine glanced up at the ceiling, contemplating the situation. "Did you know that many small communities in Alaska still use the bartering system?"

There was a long pause. Finally, Jerome said, "The one thousand dollars I owe you doesn't pay in full for this bed."

"No, but it'll pay for half. I'll make up the rest." She gave herself a mental shake. *Make up the rest? Have I lost my mind?*

On second thought, maybe this wasn't such a crazy idea. It was only a quarter of her cruise refund. Besides, a thousand dollars wouldn't save her agency—she needed a substantial loan to do that.

Jerome glanced over his shoulder. The man and woman were smiling, sort of, but inching toward the door. Turning back to Blaine, Jerome sighed. "Appears there's no sale."

Blaine glanced at her wristwatch. "Well, it's noon so you're not obligated to hold it any longer." She grinned broadly. "Jerome, wrap it up with a big bow because this baby's sold."

BLAINE BLEW A LOCK OF hair out of her eyes as she stared at the apartment door, upon which was crookedly nailed a number 4. "Jerome," Blaine muttered under her breath, "maybe you should've paid Ralph first."

Ralph swore he misheard the address where he was to deliver the brass bed, but Blaine couldn't help but wonder if Ralph was nursing a grudge that his account with Jerome was still unpaid. A really big grudge considering that when she discovered Ralph had misdelivered the bed, and asked him to redeliver it, he claimed it would cost her and Jerome double.

No way Blaine was paying double.

So, she'd decided to pick it up and deliver it herself.

She knocked. No answer. *Great. Nobody's home. Or are they?*

Frowning, she pressed her ear to the door, trying to detect any telltale squeaking brass bed sounds. Her beautiful brass bed better *not* be being broken in by some apartment dwellers turned vigorous, sex-starved sex fiends! Because that was what that bed did to people—it ignited their deepest, lustiest desires. Their magical dreams. Their secret indulgences.

That's what it'd done for Blaine, anyway.

She started to knock, but opted to pound on the door this time. "Get off that bed," she whispered in a throaty growl.

"May I help you?" asked a scratchy, feminine voice.

Blaine spun around to see a diminutive little old lady wearing a strawberry pink running outfit and white high-heeled sandals. Her brown eyes sparkled with curiosity while she puffed on a cigarette.

"Uh, my bed—I mean, my sister's bed—was delivered here by mistake and I need to pick it up."

The lady blew out a stream of blue smoke. "You mean those big, burly fellows went to all that trouble, only to deliver it to the wrong place?"

Blaine nodded, fighting the urge to sneeze. Right now, she'd opt for Jerome's cologne over cigarette smoke. Good thing she had her allergy pills with her. She'd pop another one as soon as she got near water.

"Are you going to pick up that big bed all by your little self?"

Blaine fought the urge to roll her eyes. She'd heard this all her life. At five-four, she'd been told she was too small to be on the girls' basketball team, but that was before she'd shown off her killer dunk. And in high school, neighbors were impressed when Blaine took on the household repairs to help out her newly widowed dad. And not just the wimpy repairs, like a leaking faucet or a squeaky door. One summer Blaine put a new roof on the house!

"I'm stronger than I look," she answered, for what seemed the zillionth time in her life. "Plus, I'm going to take the bed apart—" she lifted her toolbox "—and then I'll cart it down piece by piece to my truck." She motioned to the street, where her dad's bowling buddy's truck was parked at the curb. "Do you, uh, know where the person who lives here is?" If Blaine could get inside fast, she had a chance to get the bed to her sister's before it got too dark.

"Donovan's in..." The lady sucked on the cigarette as she thought. "...San Antonio, I think. Or was it San José?"

Blaine paused. "He's in *Texas* or *California?*"

The lady nodded.

"How'd he accept a delivered bed, then end up in another state so fast?"

The lady waved her cigarette in the air. "Oh, no, no, no. He's been out of town for almost a week now. *I'm* the one who let the men in to deliver the bed."

"You live here, too?" Then why were they standing outside, having this discussion?

"Oh, no, no, no. I'm Donovan's neighbor, Milly. He travels so much, he left me a key in case there's an emergency at his place, or like today, he gets a surprise delivery."

Surprise to him and me, both. "Then you can let me in so I can redeliver the bed?" Blaine fished in her pocket, pulling out both a tissue as well as the receipt. She tried to show the correct paper product to the woman. "Because, as you can see, I legally own this bed."

The lady eyed the paper and nodded. "Just one moment. I'll get the key."

Five minutes later, Blaine stood inside this Donovan person's apartment. Before heading back to her place, Milly had said to be careful of his plant.

Shifting her toolbox from one hand to another, Blaine looked around the living room. It was almost

7:00 p.m., so there was plenty of light out. But this place was *dark*.

"What kind of plant?" she muttered to herself, squinting to decipher objects in the shadows. "Potato?" She set the toolbox on the floor, crossed to the windows, and opened the drapes. Sunlight flooded in, lifting the gloom.

With a pleased sigh, Blaine turned around and paused.

"What is he? A *monk?*"

She'd never seen such a sparsely decorated place. It was almost as though no one lived here. In the far corner of the living room was a seen-better-days, plaid recliner with a standing pole lamp next to it. Against the right wall was a bookshelf, filled with hardback and paperback novels, and one shelf of CDs. On top of the bookshelf was a CD player, bracketed with two square speakers.

And no plant.

She glanced to her right. Set back, more a nook than a separate room, was the kitchen. Except for a few objects on the counter, it was white and bare.

"That's it?" she said to herself, her gaze traveling back over the apartment. "No TV?" She couldn't imagine a guy not watching sports or cop shows. Maybe he kept it in his bedroom...the room that housed her gorgeous bed.

Time to get to work. Blaine picked up her toolbox and headed for the hallway, which had two doors. One to the bathroom, one to the bedroom.

And in the latter, she saw her bed. Her beautiful, fantasy-drenched bed.

It sat in the center of the room, sparkling from the sunlight that fell in yellow slants through blinds on the window on the back wall. The streams of light fired spots of gold and copper on the brass. Blaine just had to stop and take in an appreciative breath at the sheer majesty of it.

She sneezed. Pulling another tissue from her pocket, she swiped at her nose and glanced again at the window. Sure enough, it was cracked open.

Enough to let in a flood of pollen.

Time to pop another allergy pill.

She typically took only one a day, but today she'd taunted the pollen gods by spending the better part of this afternoon outside—walking to Jerome's, walking to the travel agency to cash in her ticket, hanging outside Henry's, her dad's buddy's, to borrow the pickup. Which had no air-conditioning, so she'd driven over here with the window rolled down.

But before taking more medicine, she wanted to quickly scope out the bed, see how it was assembled.

She headed toward the magical, sexy object.

Crackle.

She looked down. She'd stepped on some big leaf.

In her mind, she heard Milly's raspy voice. "Be careful of his plant."

Blaine gingerly lifted her foot and eyed the humongous leaf. Had to be the size of a dinner plate. Her gaze traveled to where it was attached to a vine that curled along the floorboard to the far corner of the room.

There, it led up to a clay pot, that housed some Jack-and-the-Beanstalk number with more leafy vines that coiled up the wall and along the top of the window.

That's no plant. That's a roommate.

Blaine leaned over, and ever so gently, pushed the vine closer to the floorboard so there'd be no more accidental steppages. She momentarily pondered how the delivery guys hadn't destroyed part of the plant, which only made Blaine feel all the guiltier for stepping on it.

Well, just because I could play sports didn't mean I was coordinated in everyday life. How many times had she knocked over a vase or tracked mud and dirt into the house?

Setting down her toolbox, she swiped at her suddenly watering eyes.

Damn allergies. She needed to *see* before she could even scope. She'd take a pill and hope it kicked in fast. With the way she was feeling, she'd wanted to postpone this bed delivery adventure, but she had to take care of it today because Sonja had hinted about all kinds of maid-of-honor and sisterly tasks up until Saturday, the day of the wedding.

Blaine retraced her steps to the kitchen. There, she opened several cupboards, which were more sparse than the rest of this guy's apartment. A few plates, bowls, cups and water glasses. She filled a glass with tap water, then retrieved her plastic vial from her shirt pocket. Tapping out a pill, she popped it into her mouth and washed it down.

On the way back to the bedroom, an object on the

bookshelf caught her eye. She paused and picked it up. An old, chipped pocket knife. *Why keep an old tool around?* She loved her tools the way other girls loved clothes and makeup. And one of her pet rules was to keep her tools in mint condition, clean and ready to use. She'd never keep an old, battered pocketknife.

Blaine turned the knife over in her hands. Besides the plant, this object seemed to be the only decoration in this place.

Placing it back on the shelf where she found it, Blaine headed back to the bedroom, yawning.

For the next fifteen minutes, she checked out how the bed was bolted together. Then she opened her toolbox and extracted a wrench.

Sleepy. I'm so sleepy.

Blinking, she positioned the wrench around the bolt. She yawned again, a long tired yawn. This wrench felt so heavy. Her eyelids felt heavier. The medication was unusually strong.

Foggily, she thought back. She took one pill after buying the bed. Another before driving Henry's truck over here. And one a few minutes ago.

Ohhhhh. Instead of her usual one, she had inadvertently taken *three.*

Distant thunder broke the silence.

An oncoming summer storm. The rain would be great, but the preceding winds would only kick up more pollen. She could already smell the ragweed, the flowers, the...

Ah-chooo!

She extracted her tissue and blew her nose.

When will that last pill kick in? Better take a breather, rest, wait for the storm to pass.

Besides, if she tried to keep working on this bed in her druggy state, she'd undoubtedly keel over on that plant and do far more than simply crunch a leaf.

Blaine hoisted herself on top of the bed. Ahhhhhh. This mattress was so big and soft, it was like sitting on a cloud. A sensuous, seductive cloud that promised a world of fantasy and dreams come true...

Too hot to sleep in my clothes. She began tugging off her T-shirt.

A few minutes later, Blaine fell back, barely aware of her head hitting the pillow.

2

THE TAXI DROVE AWAY, its motor fading into the night air as Donovan Roy unlocked the door. A breeze riffled the air, infusing it with the rich scent of earth and grass. *Must have rained earlier.* He was partial to this time of year in Colorado, when an afternoon storm could rush in like a giddy schoolgirl, all breathless and flustered, then unleash its passion like a seasoned woman.

He shifted his overnight bag on his shoulder, catching another scent. Roses. Or was it honeysuckle? No, that had been in San José. Lilacs? Could be. They'd grown in wild abundance, purple and fragrant, outside his hotel room in Cincinnati.

San José.

Cincinnati.

As he shoved the door open with his shoulder, his thoughts struggled. Which city was he in this time?

His memory was always sharp, damn near perfect, except when he pushed himself, mentally and physically, to the limit. *Shouldn't have taken this last job. Should have taken a break.* But he'd needed the money.

He paused on the threshold, squinting at the shadows in the room.

Hell, it's home!

He kicked shut the door behind him and dropped

his bag, which hit the hardwood floor with a solid whoomp. He tugged off one of his boots and tossed it next to the bag.

God, I'm wiped.

He reminded himself that despite such dog-tired moments, he liked doing what he wanted, where he wanted, when he wanted. Liked keeping his boots next to the front door, liked tossing back a shot while listening to the blues, liked keeping the ringer on his phone permanently off.

Which was why he liked his consulting gigs. They fit his lifestyle to a T. No playing the corporate games, no molding himself to society's expectations. As long as he met his deadlines and produced quality work, he could wear his hair longer, dress in jeans and T-shirts, take off a few days when the mood struck.

He yanked off the other boot, then remained bent over, arching his back to release some tension. His body ached from folding his six-three frame into airline seats, taxi seats. This past year, he swore he'd visited more cities than the president himself. *Wonder if it's the same for the big guy—* After a while, people and cities blurred into a swirl of shapes and voices.

Especially when Donovan pulled an all-nighter, like he'd done last night in San José.

He straightened, tossing the other boot in the vicinity of the first, then glanced up at the clock on his wall. A slant of moonlight highlighted the chunk of redwood he'd found on the California coast several years ago. Inspired, he'd polished and rigged it to be a clock.

3:00 a.m.

Donovan scratched the stubble on his chin. He'd been up—he squeezed shut his eyes and added the numbers—damn, over forty hours.

His eyes suddenly felt gritty, heavy. Sleep didn't beckon, it badgered. He absently rubbed his right leg, the damn spot that ached when he pushed his body too hard.

Gotta get to bed. I'll sleep till noon, maybe later, then make myself the meanest, hottest plate of huevos rancheros this side of the border.

Smiling at the prospect, he trudged toward the hallway as he peeled off his T-shirt. Reaching the recliner, gray and bulky in the shadows, he tossed the shirt over its back. Then he stripped off his jeans, stepped out of his briefs, and dropped both on the floor.

With a drawn-out yawn, he headed for the bedroom. He started to roll over onto the mattress, but it was...different. He fumbled in the dark. Damn, this mattress was higher off the ground than he recalled. A good foot, maybe two, higher.

He was so tired, it took all his will to keep the shadowy dream figures that toyed at the edges of his consciousness at bay. So tired, the thump-thump of the old pine tree that brushed the side of this apartment building whenever the winds got restless, sounded eerily like the drumbeat of an old Muddy Waters song.

Donovan blinked his heavy eyelids. Too heavy to stay open.

So why in the hell am I still standing?

Oh yeah, the bed. Too high.

He stroked the satiny mattress cover. Felt like that bed at the motel in Cincinnati. Or was it Seattle?

Hell, that's where he probably was. Cincinnati or Seattle or...

He lifted his good leg, rolled onto the mattress, and stretched out his tired body. Ah, the breezes felt good. Warm. Comforting. Like a woman's touch...

The shadowy figures in his mind sharpened and withdrew, preparing to start the dream.

Silky strands of hair caressed his cheek. The scent of soap and almonds.

Almonds. Reminded him of Deidre, the airline stewardess in Boston, and her almond-scented body lotion. He flashed on her raven hair, blue eyes...he couldn't remember much more. Their hit-and-miss relationship had been a long time ago...another lifetime ago...

The image faded.

His leg brushed against another, feminine one.

Yeah, let me dream of a lady.

In the dark haze of his mind, he imagined his fingers touching warm skin. Soft. Supple. As he explored the feminine curve of a back, he was vaguely aware of other sensations.

Warm, dewy skin.

Smooth, taut muscle.

Scented breezes, imbued with a hint of almonds, swirled around them, enveloped them.

Oh, yeah, let the dream come on.

He willingly let his mind slip over the edge of reality into a haze.

The woman liquefied in his arms, her shape conforming to his. He stretched to his full length, relishing the fluidity of curves and bends that molded against his primed body.

Breasts, soft and full, pressed against him. The puckered tips of nipples tightened, grew hard.

Feeling her arousal was like an aphrodisiac.

His fingers explored the terrain. He ran a palm, fingers spread wide, down a taut tummy, played briefly with a navel, then reversed course and crept back up to the soft, round base of a breast.

He stretched open his fingers even wider, sliding them on either side of a pebbled nipple. With a groan, he rolled the nub between his fingers, tugging it gently.

A feminine moan. Ragged, breathy. And when her hips ground a little against him, desire shot through him like a bolt of lightning.

His hand slipped down, instinctively seeking that spot of heat and gratification...

In her dream, Blaine sat on a chair, staring across the cruise deck at Mount McKinley, which rose like a foreboding monolith to a sky filled with pristine white clouds. So white, it pained her eyes to stare at it.

Cool sea breezes ruffled her hair.

No, fingers ruffled her hair.

She blinked, groggily aware that the sunlight had faded to black. Hazily aware that the wild and rugged Alaskan terrain had disappeared.

The dream had shifted, changed.

She was naked, in the arms of a man.

She felt mesmerized by his warmth and masculine scent. His solid body crushed her close. So close, she couldn't tell where her skin ended, where his began. It was as though they were one warm, pulsating body.

She shuddered a breath, falling further into the dream. Relinquishing herself to it.

As their bodies shifted, her skin burned and tingled at points where they touched.

She moaned.

A deep, throaty groan responded.

A soothing breeze swept over them. The scent of pine. A dream took shape. Instead of a cruise ship, she lay beneath a tree, the swaying branches sweeping a blue sky. Sweeping, stroking her skin...

...no, the man's hand stroked her skin. Down, down...brushing the bend of her waist, inching up her torso and sliding over her breast.

She gasped and pressed herself into his warm palm. Flames fanned higher as his fingers played lazily around her breast, circling the nipple. Rough, yet sensuous hands. And oh, so sweet the way they moved magically over her skin. Stroking, caressing, teasing...

Heat swept over her body, then sank through her skin, flooding every cell with a primitive need.

The hand slipped away.

The dream suspended. Savage disappointment shot through her.

His hand wedged between her legs.

Then he touched her *there*.

The world shrank to a focal point of fiery need where his fingers circled and stroked her sex. She tensed, arching her back, aching for release.

Hot, wet lips suckled her breast and she emitted a soft, guttural cry.

Wave after wave of heat rushed through her. She needed...more. Maneuvering her pelvis just *so*, she sank herself onto those skilled fingers.

Sizzling need coiled within Donovan as velvety heat enveloped his fingers, which mimicked what other parts of him wanted to do.

Against his chest, he felt feathery shudders of breath.

And where he touched her. God, that was the sweetest. Her hips thrust against him with a small yearning movement that spread fire through his body.

Need skyrocketed through him. Unbearable, exquisite need.

Shadows, like flames, leapt and danced in the periphery of his dream.

He tugged her snug against him, took his hardened member and slid it into her. God...so...tight. She was so wet, so ready. He shifted his hips, inching farther into silky, feminine folds.

She moaned, the sound sweet and anxious.

He slipped deeper until he was fully inside, his desire straining as he fought the urge to explode...to tumble over the edge...

Her body stiffened. A strangled gasp escalated to a cry as her insides contracted, tighter, tighter...

He stilled, holding her against him, as though they were poised on the edge of the world.

And as her insides suddenly convulsed, he buried himself into her, exploding his release.

BLAINE BLINKED. Sunshine, bright and hot, fell across her face. Hundreds of dust particles swayed and danced in the shaft of dazzling light. She sucked in a breath and coughed.

Damn allergies. She sniffed. Double damn. She was hopelessly clogged up.

And hopelessly groggy.

After rubbing her watery eyes, she again squinted into the sunshine. Above her head, a window was open.

No wonder she could hardly breathe—all the pollens in Manitou Springs had probably found their way through that opening last night. Two months ago, when she'd rented this room, her dad had warned her about living in a stranger's house. *People will use your things without asking. People won't respect the ten-to-six rule.* The latter being one of her dad's favorites as long as she could remember—the "ten-to-six" rule being that you turned down the noise from 10:00 p.m. to 6:00 a.m. so people could sleep.

But she'd just chalked up his warnings to his worrisome nature.

Except for this morning. Somebody had sneaked into her room and opened her window. That went far beyond simply breaking the ten-to-six rule. That was breaking her fundamental, I need-to-breathe-it's-allergy-season rule.

Although which of her roommates would open her window was a mystery. Georgio, who's real name was George but "Georgio" better fit his flamboyant hairdresser persona, owned the house. But his master bedroom and bath were at the far end of the house and he never entered her room unannounced. Which left the other paying renter, Sam, a sullen college student whose wardrobe consisted of jeans and *Star Wars* T-shirts and who seemed to subsist on cigarettes and coffee.

Not that Sam seemed like a stealthy window opener, but those Trekkie types sometimes did odd things. She once walked in while Sam and some of his buddies were mixing green Jell-O in the bathtub.

Her gaze shifted to a section of glistening metal below the window. Glistening, cylindrical brass that magically looped and curled.

My beloved bed!

Well, Sonja's bed.

Blaine smiled lazily and stretched.

Wait. How'd my bed get into my tiny, cramped rent-a-room?

She frowned, vaguely recalling crawling into the bed after too many allergy pills. *Well, no wonder I'm having a heck of a time waking up.* She strained to remember exactly what happened last night. Images slowly materialized in her sluggish brain. Henry's truck, Milly, a big leaf...

More images took shape in her mind. Not images exactly, but sensations.

Big, rough hands. Bare skin against bare skin. Roaming, skilled fingers...

A sleepy, and very masculine, groan interrupted her mental inventory.

Someone, no some *man,* was behind her, on the other side of the bed!

She stiffened, terrified she'd look over her shoulder and discover one of Sam's Trekkie friends, wearing thick horn-rim glasses, a Jedi outfit and reeking of green Jell-O. God, had she done it with a Trekkie?

She squeezed shut her eyes. *Please, Lord, I wanted to be Liv Tyler, not Princess Leia.*

She stealthily eased herself off the bed, nearly falling when her foot lost traction on the slick satin-covered mattress. She caught herself, then wobbled to a standing position.

With great trepidation, she turned and looked at her mattress mate.

A guy's long, muscular, tan body was sprawled naked across the white satin mattress.

Naked. She glanced around the room. Good. No Jedi or Vader gear. Better yet, no Jell-O.

She eased out a pent-up breath, coughing slightly in the process. This room...she eyed the plant, suddenly remembering exactly where she was. This is that traveling guy's apartment. Where the bed had been misdelivered.

She tilted her head and checked him out. Was this the traveling man? What had Milly said his name was?

Blaine rubbed her itchy eyes as more hot, fuzzy memories of lusty sex coalesced in her mind. She dropped her hands and stared at the guy...the guy she'd...noooo, impossible. *I'm a practical, hardworking rule follower—I'm the last person to have hot sex with a stranger!*

That was the kind of thing her sister Sonja might have done, but *never* Blaine. No, Blaine was the one to whom Sonja made such confessions, not the one who committed the deeds. And Sonja had confessed some doozies to her big sis Blaine, who tried to listen with a straight face and an open mind while also amazed at what two people could do with too much time, and lust, on their hands.

And now Blaine had joined this too-much-time, over-lusted segment of society.

She frowned. What *exactly* had they done?

More memories. Sweat-drenched bodies and a moment of pleasure so intense, so exquisite...

She wiped her suddenly shaky hand across her moist brow. Those memories were too real. They must have done exactly what she feared they'd done.

And it all happened on her wedding gift to her sister.

Blaine shut her eyes, giving her head a shake. *Forget the bed, you have bigger issues to deal with.* You don't even know this guy's history, much less his sexual history.

How many times had she counseled Sonja on this very subject. Badgered her about using protection.

Okay, I need to figure out who this guy is, make sure he's...healthy, then get this damn bed moved.

Blaine did an inventory of her mystery lover. Thick brown hair that curled at his temples and neck.

She tugged mindlessly at her own shoulder-length hair. *Wonder if he doesn't have enough money for a haircut these days, either.*

His eyes were closed, which accentuated the fringe

of thick lashes that skirted his lids. Coarse brown stubble roughened the lower half of his face.

And what a face.

Square, solid, with a chin that jutted forward slightly even as he slept. As though on guard, ready to take life on the chin. *A tough guy.* Funny, though, how he slept with his hands clenched into tight balls, as though he were protecting something. What? From what she'd seen of his place, he owned next to nothing. Maybe he was protecting something deep inside himself. A secret.

Her gaze swept back over him. He was tall, if she judged the way his head touched one end of the mattress and his feet almost dangled off the other.

She perused him head to foot again, stopping in the middle... Maybe this was crass, but she wanted a good look for herself, ensure that he looked healthy before she woke him up and asked him if he was.

He looked good. Very good. Normal. No, better than normal, but that wasn't what she was supposed to be checking.

She released a pent-up breath.

But she'd have to be blind not to notice.

Even asleep, with his body relaxed, he was *big.* Not that she was a size expert, unless intimate relationships with four different men—well, technically three— made one an expert. Which, at thirty years of age, was an embarrassing admission.

"What are you staring at?" asked a gruff, irritated male voice.

Donovan blinked at the naked woman, who slowly

raised her head and stared, wide-eyed, her green eyes nearly translucent in a slant of bright yellow sunlight. It reminded him of the way sunlight filtered through the aquamarine waters in the Caribbean. The rays sliced through those shimmering blue waters, revealing every nuance of life.

She quickly crossed her arms so they covered her breasts—but not before he'd seen their full, pink-tipped beauty. A memory seared through his mind, then faded.

Her mouth opened, then shut, then opened again. "I'm...I'm..." Suddenly, she dropped back her head, then jerked forward with an ear-numbing sneeze.

He shut his eyes. Gave his head a shake.

He'd woken up bone weary plenty of times before, but it'd been years since he'd woken up with a woman he didn't even recognize.

And of the two or three fair members of the opposite sex with whom he had woken up and not remembered, this was the first who'd checked out his privates, then sneezed.

He'd try not to read too much into that.

He scrubbed a hand over his face, then squinted open one eye. Coffee. He needed coffee.

He glanced up. She stood there, cross-armed and wide-eyed. As though she were standing at attention.

"What are you doing?" he croaked.

She shrugged. "Waitink..." She coughed, then cleared her throat. "Waiting for you to wake up," she answered, enunciating each word.

"Well, I'm up." Barely. He never dealt with the

world, especially the people in it, until after he'd had his jolt of caffeine. The opposite of this lady, it appeared, who bounded out of bed and observed the world—and those still sleeping in it—with big, disarming green eyes.

With great effort, he propped himself on his elbow, determined not be amused by this quirky situation. He still wasn't sure what he was dealing with, but whatever it was, he'd keep his cool until he understood the situation, which was a one-eighty turn from the younger, hotheaded Donovan.

"You sick?" he asked.

"Allergies."

Naked. Wild auburn hair. Allergies.

And, he thought with an inward smile, impossibly cute.

But nothing clicked. Not a single detail, and he a man who earned good money thanks to his affinity for details. Couldn't analyze a computer failure unless one had a head for bits and bytes.

And nibbles. Another flash of memory. His lips on her flesh, nibbling.

He squinted one eye at her. For the life of him, he was clueless to identify this emerald-eyed, allergy-ridden woman who stood naked before him.

And if he couldn't identify her, could he identify where the hell they were?

He jerked his head around.

He was in some fancy brass bed, for starters. He glanced around the room. White, nondescript walls. And his plant.

He frowned and looked up at the slatted blinds, with the missing fourth slat that always looked like a missing tooth. *And that's my window.* He shifted his gaze back to the intruder.

"What the hell are you doing in my bedroom?" Okay, so much for keeping his cool. This was *his* turf. Different rules altogether. Nobody entered his domain, *ever*, without his permission. Maybe he'd lost a lot in the world, but he still owned his privacy.

Without moving her strategically placed arms, she managed to point a forefinger at the bed. "This belongth to me."

He paused, unprepared for that curve ball. "This...bed," he repeated slowly.

She nodded.

"This bed that's in *my* bedroom."

She nodded, her eyes widening.

He should count to ten. "Tell me." One, two, three. "How the hell did *your* bed get into *my* bedroom?"

"Rawlf," she whispered, followed by a cough.

His gaze slid down, over her arms—*for a compact type, she's got some biceps*—down to her belly button, which is where the mattress cut off his view. Nothing *looked* familiar, yet heated memories of satiny skin and soft breasts ricocheted through his mind.

Had they...?

He glanced down. He was naked, too. Not that he really gave a damn. Growing up on a ranch with three older, rowdy brothers had permanently eradicated his shy gene.

But considering *he* was naked, and *she* was naked...

He cocked an eyebrow and shot her a look. He caught her scent. *Sweet, like almonds.* That little detail sizzled through his brain, triggering other memories. The taste of her lips. Her lusty moan.

Details...small details taunted his memory. If he didn't need the money so bad, he'd blow off future back-to-back business trips. Because to forget what you experienced with a woman had to be one sorry statement for a man's life.

First things first. "Where's *my* bed?"

Her plump little lips opened into a little O—and remained stuck in that position. Finally, she blurted, "*Your* bed?"

Back in college, this would have been one of his buddies' tricks. Plant a naked woman and a strange bed in good ol' Donnie's room. But he didn't have buddies like that anymore. Had no buddies, actually, unless he counted Bill, the bartender at The Keg.

"My bed. Wooden. Plain." He'd never described his bed before, just slept in it. It was comfortable, cheap...and up until last night, reliable.

She wriggled her nose, as though she were going to sneeze again, then pursed her lips and appeared to hold her breath for a long moment. Finally, she released her breath in a whoosh, looking relieved. "Don't know."

He nodded. *Forget the coffee, I'll just go straight for the vodka.* But despite the insanity of the situation, he detected a logical thread. "Did Rawlf take it?"

She cleared her throat. "R-A-L-P-H," she spelled.

"Oh, *Ralph*." It was hard to stay ticked listening to

such a cute, stuffed-up nose. Attached to such a cute, compact body. He rubbed his bottom lip, trying not to smile. "So did, uh, Ralph take it?"

"Prob'bly," she answered.

Donovan dragged his hands through his hair, blew out a gust of air, then shoved himself across the bed. He swung his legs over and stood in front of Ms. Big Green Eyes. Her female scent wove around him, drugging him with more eerily familiar sensations of heat and sin....

He gave his head a shake, forcing his thoughts to stay focused on the problem at hand.

Although part of him didn't feel this was such a big problem anymore. Hell, it'd been so long since he'd had fun, he almost didn't recognize the feeling. It was almost like being the old Donnie again, enjoying the moment, feeling alive....

"I take it Ralph then delivered this bed and picked up my bed—although you're still a big question mark." He stepped closer.

Her green eyes darkened, as though a shadow had passed over a sparkling sea. And in that moment, he realized this woman was nervous about whatever had happened between them. Not shy-nervous, but anxious-nervous as though she was in way over her head. To look at her strong little body, she appeared to be a woman who could handle anything.

But that look in her eyes betrayed a fragility.

The realization stabbed him, right to the core of a memory he wished he could forget. He knew how people could appear strong, yet be so fragile that when they shattered, pieces of their life splintered far and wide, some never to be found again.

"I guess Milly can fill in the details," he said quietly. Only his neighbor Milly could have let these people in. And she would have had a good reason. Yeah, she'd explain everything...except why and how this woman got naked...

Another steamy memory burned through his brain. Too real, too hot to be merely a dream. He reached over and touched the woman's hair. The silky strands fell through his fingers...a sensation he recalled from last night...

"Did we—?" he asked. "Are we—?"

Her eyes moistened as though she couldn't contain her feelings any longer. She nodded, her chin trembling.

"We're...we're..." A tear spilled down her cheek. "...lubbers."

3

"LUBBERS?" DONOVAN ASKED, cocking an eyebrow.

She swallowed, hard. "Lubbers," she said slowly.

He noticed she was breathing through her mouth. Allergies. Then it hit him. "Lovers," he repeated slowly.

She closed and opened her eyes, then nodded sadly.

Was I that bad? Maybe he hadn't been with a woman in a while—okay, months—but that didn't mean he'd lost his touch. Hey, once you learned how to ride a bike, you never forgot, right?

Which somebody needed to remind this lady.

"Let's get dressed," he growled, turning around, "then discuss this bed situation."

She coughed. "Question."

He paused. "What?"

"Are you...healthy?"

"What?" Coffee. Black, hot, *now*.

"Healthy." She coughed again. "You know, no diseases or anyting."

Then it dawned on him what she meant. They hadn't used...damn, he never did that. If he hadn't been so exhausted.

"I'm healthy. Just had my annual. I'm a hundred

percent." He paused. "You?" After all, he should ask, too.

She snorted. "Very, *very* healthy." She coughed.

"For the record, except for last night, I always use protection with a woman. I don't know what happened..." It was the truth. Honest to God, he thought it was a dream.

"I don't know what happened, either."

Well, at least she was taking partial responsibility. "Now that we've covered that, let's get dressed."

Heading out of the room, he spied a red toolbox and a pile of clothes in the corner of the bedroom.

"Those yours?" he said, glancing over his shoulder. She quickly covered her breasts and nodded.

"You missed one." He dropped his gaze to a dark pink nipple that peeked through two of her fingers.

She gave a little shriek, fumbling to cover up.

He turned away, smiling to himself. "I'll get dressed in the living room. You get dressed in here. Let's meet up in five and discuss what happened to our beds. And how you ended up in my house."

But they'd skip the part about how they also ended up becoming "lubbers." Hell, what *had* happened? He'd sworn it was a steamy, erotic dream where everything fit just *right*. Reality was never like that. Not the first time, anyway. He'd never taken a woman to bed and instinctively known her body. Known its terrain as well as his own. Known where to touch, how much pressure, when she was ready. That's why it had seemed so...perfect. As though they were destined to be lovers.

Perfect?

Destined?

Hell, he was sounding like a guy who'd fallen in love at first sight. Hit by a zap of lightning. The kind of crock those New Age poets that dawdled at the Spice of Life coffee shop spent hours scribbling about. They'd sit for hours sipping their chai tea, writing love poems on napkins while listening to piped-in harp music.

Buddy, you're still suffering from sleep deprivation. You need coffee. Hot, black, and kick-ass strong.

Naked, he marched to the kitchen.

BLAINE BLEW ON THE COFFEE. It was too hot to drink, smelled like burnt beans and was black enough to fill a fountain pen. But she accepted it, with a smile, because it was the least she could do after throwing a wrench into this guy's life. Plus she wanted to be as easy to get along with as possible considering she'd intruded on his life, his *bed*. Well, her bed.

She cringed inwardly. *Argghhh. If only I hadn't overdosed on that allergy medicine last night.* Because if she hadn't, she wouldn't have woken up without a stitch, next to a royally pissed-off guy whose bed she'd somehow lost.

She stifled a sneeze. Great, her allergies were acting up again, but no way in hell would she pop a pill. Not right now, anyway. Even though one pill never made her that sleepy, after her little overdose yesterday, she didn't want to take another one too soon. The last thing she needed was to fall asleep while he was talking to her and further test that thundercloud mood he'd flashed earlier.

At least this time, they were both dressed. And this room had some light in it, thanks to the opened curtain and switched-on lamp. She glanced to her right. Yesterday, she'd noticed the books, but had been unable to see their titles. Now she could clearly see the words on their spines. A biography of Ulysses Grant, another of Robert E. Lee. Novels like *The Razor's Edge, Of Human Bondage.* A thick book titled *Great Poets of the Twentieth Century.*

No thrillers? Mysteries? Man, this guy went for the heavy stuff. She wondered if that reflected his life, too. Heavy books, heavy thinkers. Which probably meant he approached situations with heavy caution.

Well, she'd certainly blown that approach sky-high!

She blew on her coffee again, more for something to do, and sneaked a peek at him over the rim of her mug. He wore a pair of faded jeans, ripped at one knee, and an olive-green T-shirt that read As You Ramble On Through Life, Brother/Whatever Be Your Goal/Keep Your Eye Upon the Doughnut/And Not Upon the Hole.

Considering his moodiness, she'd have thought he kept his eye upon the hole.

He took a slug of coffee. She cringed inwardly as she watched him swallow the stuff. *His gut must be made of asbestos.*

"Start from the top," he said, leaning back in the recliner.

He'd been sitting on his recliner when she'd finally

emerged, fully dressed, from the bedroom. Surprisingly, he offered her a cup of coffee *and* the recliner, which had left her momentarily dumbstruck. She'd expected the guy to blast her with some angry accusations, not polite inquiries.

Rugged, moody...yet, it appeared a heart beat within the beast.

She'd accepted the coffee. And declined the recliner—after all, it was the only place to sit in the room, and who was she to deny a man his throne? So, she'd sat cross-legged on the hardwood floor. As she got comfortable, she'd noticed he rubbed his leg again. Funny, he didn't appear to have a limp, but then the only time she'd seen him walk was when he exited the bedroom, butt-naked.

And to be honest, her eyes hadn't been focused on his legs at that moment.

"From the top?" he prompted.

Oh, yeah, he'd asked her a question. "Frob de top?" she repeated. Damn allergies. She was starting to sound like a clogged pipe. *Keep it short and sweet.*

She sucked in some air through her mouth. "Yesterday, I cashed id my Alaskan cruise ticket ad bought by sister a bed." She paused to catch a breath. "A weddig gift frob me." That was neat and tidy. No mention of boyfriends getting engaged or the pending bank loan...

There was a long pause during which the guy frowned, downing another slug of coffee. She could tell by the glint in his eyes that his mind was working, the wheels turning. Oh yeah, he was cautious all right.

When he finally nodded, Blaine realized it had taken all that time to decipher what she'd said.

"And?" he prompted.

"And...de bed was delivered to de wrog address."

"Rog?"

She nodded.

"Oh, *wrong*."

She fought the urge to roll her eyes. This guy was serious to the max. The last thing she needed to do was make light of the situation.

"Delivered to the wrong address by this Ralph person."

"Yes." She tried to down a sip of coffee, but the stuff damn near scalded her tongue. She sucked in a cooling breath of air, her eyes watering. "How do you drik this stuff?"

"I like hot things."

Heat flooded her face. That's what last night had been. Hot. The hottest she'd *ever* experienced. God, her skin burned with the memory of his touch. Those calloused hands were skilled, relentless...

She looked around the room, too embarrassed to meet this guy's eyes...her *lover's* eyes. She shifted, trying to find a more comfortable position on the floor. Man, she was sweating in places she'd never sweated in before. Memories of what happened last night—in her sister's *wedding-present bed*, for God's sake—were better than anything, *anything*, Blaine had ever experienced with a guy, which now just seemed a blur of fumbling and body parts.

Maybe it had been better because last night had been like...a fantasy. Lush, provocative, *meltdown hot*.

Maybe that bed was magical, after all.

She looked up at the man with whom she'd shared the ultimate intimacy—what had Milly called him?

"What's your nameb?" she asked.

He frowned. "Oh, *name*. Donovan. Donovan Roy."

His finger played along the lip of his cup, circling it slowly. "Yours?"

"Blaind Saudders," she answered, forcing herself to look him in the eyes and not at his finger, whose sensuous, circling motion reminded her of how he'd touched her last night. "I rud de Blaind Saudders Temp Agency."

He stared at her, his brow furrowed. "Okay," he said slowly.

His last name rang a bell. "Roy's Eggs?"

He seemed to hesitate before answering. "My mom sells those, yes," he said gruffly. A shadow crossed his features.

He took another drink of coffee, but seemed to keep the mug in front of his face afterward. As though not wanting to face something?

Not face Blaine? Uh-oh, and here she was, savoring last night's sensuous finger play while he was analyzing his great escape. Maybe this was one of those dreaded "morning-afters" she'd heard Sonja and her girlfriends talk about. The guy's uncomfortable, afraid the woman doesn't know the difference between a fling and forevermore, and he's dumb-ass clueless how to deal with it.

Blaine looked down at the scuffed hardwood floor. *Shame. I could sand and varnish this, make it shine like new.*

"So," she finally whispered, "when de bed could't be redelivered, I decided to do it byself." There. She was picking up their previous thread of conversation, saving him from having to deal with whatever-it-was-that-happened-between-them last night.

"I see."

Donovan searched Blaine's face so long, she had the eerie sense he read beneath her words, sensed her feelings. And for a moment, she despised him for it. Wanted to tell him, in no uncertain terms, that she wasn't wondering some girly thing like "will he call me?" That *she* didn't pine and daydream over *any* guy...

"Milly let you in."

"You have a problem with dat?" Blaine snapped. Some of her coffee sloshed onto the floor. Bending over, she wiped it up with the sleeve of her T-shirt.

"No," he said slowly, looking at the smeared brown stain on her T-shirt. "Milly has a key. I've told her to use it when necessary." He paused. "You didn't have to do that. I have paper towels, you know."

"I know." She slugged back a mouthful of hot coffee, wincing as she swallowed.

"You okay?"

She nodded, afraid to speak. Sometimes even she was aware she was behaving oddly, but damn if she was going to let *him* know that.

After a long moment, he continued, "I'm still trying to understand why you decided to sleep in my bed."

Decided? As though she'd planned this little escapade? She bit her tongue, reminding herself that her bed—her gorgeous, magical bed—was at stake. She needed to stay reasonable and calm because the bed was now in this guy's possession. And wasn't possession nine-tenths of the law?

"Allergy pills," she said softly. "Too many. Fell asleep." She expelled a weighty breath, which unfortunately came out as a scratchy wheeze.

"You sound terrible."

"I am terrible." She winced. Maybe she was trying to be calm and reasonable, but it didn't mean her tongue didn't move ahead of her mind sometimes. Okay, so she felt bad about what had happened. Not such an awful thing for this guy to know.

One corner of his mouth kicked up in a grin. "No, you're not."

"I like to follow the rules."

His eyes sparkled. "Could've fooled me." He took another slug of his coffee. After swallowing, he said. "Myself, I abhor rules. Maybe you should rethink your stance, be easier on yourself."

This wasn't at all what she expected. Rather than ranting and raving at her, he wanted to talk, so she was talking—or trying to. And in return, the guy was acting interested, heck, even sounding concerned.

As though he cares.

Her insides went all swampy. And the way he looked at her—his rugged face softening, those full lips giving her a loose, kicked-up grin, made her feel... special.

Guys often looked at her kid sister this way. Blaine knew because she'd seen it plenty of times. And she never begrudged her sister for it, either. It was part of being the surrogate mom, happy for Sonja's beauty and popularity. Thankful, even, because Blaine knew life would be easier for Sonja. It wasn't a bad thing, just a reality. Some people stood a bit more in life's golden light.

But at this moment, Blaine suddenly had an inkling of what it was like to bask in that light. To feel... cherished.

She swiped at the corner of her eye, hoping Donovan thought it was allergies, not emotion, getting to her. *Damn, I'm getting all girly. If this guy doesn't cut to the chase, wrap up business, I'll have to do it myself.*

"I didn't take advantage of you."

She looked up. "Huh?"

"Last night. I didn't take advantage of you."

She peered at him, momentarily taken aback by his admission. He looked so...apologetic.

"I, uh, was tired." He rubbed that spot on his leg again. "Had been up for hours. Days, actually." He dragged a hand through his hair. "Honest to God, I thought I was dreaming. I'd never take advantage of a woman."

Dreaming. He thought he was dreaming. *It had nothing to do with me.* She plastered on a smile. "Do't worry," she said, forcing herself to sound upbeat, confident.

"What's Ralph's number?" Donovan stood, dangling the empty coffee mug off one finger.

Blaine started to look at his face, but all that body was in the way. Her gaze did a slow tour up his jean-clad legs, past that midriff, which underneath that T-shirt she knew to be tight, muscled, and covered with a wild mass of hair.

Finally, she reached his face—solid, angled—and peered into those soft brown eyes. Funny, back in the bedroom, when their conversation had been tense, those eyes had been a turbulent brown—like a dirty, churning river during a winter deluge.

Now they spilled light, the muddy brown shifting to a whiskey color.

"Ralph's number?" he repeated.

"Od my desk." Jerome had called her at work and left it. She'd jotted it on one of her sticky notes.

Donovan headed toward the kitchen. "Is he listed?"

She couldn't remember Ralph's last name. "My friend who sold me da bed has da numbbb—" she blew out an exasperated breath, tired of being so damn clogged up "—number." There, she got the word out.

"Got your friend's number?"

Blaine looked at those whiskey eyes. This was a man who took care of business, no matter what was churning inside of him. She could relate to that. "Sure," she answered.

A few minutes later, after talking briefly with Jerome, Donovan was punching in Ralph's number on a kitchen wall phone, its blue color dull, its receiver scarred with what looked to be a burn mark. But old, usable things seemed to be Donovan's style. The old, torn plaid recliner. Makeshift bookshelf, really a carefully arranged assortment of old cement bricks and two-by-fours.

Donovan glanced at her where she sat perched on a plastic kitchen chair, which she'd guessed was formerly someone's patio furniture. "I think he owes us one free delivery."

"Thik again."

"No sweat. I can be cool during difficult negotiations."

Negotiations? What did Donovan do for a living? Whatever it was, he couldn't make much money. Her college student roommate had more furniture than Donovan.

"Ralph?" Donovan winked at Blaine.

Winked? *He probably winks at everyone. Part of his "cool" negotiating style.* But, whatever it was, she loved it. Could eat it with a spoon. She wiggled her toes, loving the giddy feeling of just hanging in the kitchen, being the lucky recipient of little side winks. This was too cool. So unlike anything that ever happened to Blaine. It was like being blindsided with...

With love?

Naahhhh. Just 'cause last night's passion felt oh-so-right—and 'cause she'd been flashed a wink—didn't mean they'd been zapped with love. There was all that other stuff that had happened, like accidentally losing his bed.

I'm probably so giddy to have a single moment where I'm not fretting over my business, that I equate a little hotsie-totsie to love. Anyway, instantly falling in love stuff only happened in the movies. Or to people in another generation. Not to practical, rule-minded Blaine.

"Donovan Roy," the object of her toe-wriggling moment said into the receiver. "Hey, it appears you delivered a bed to my address." He paused. "Well, it's the wrong address. Uh-huh. Uh-huh. Not your fault. I see. Well, friend, I have a dilemma. Do you know what happened to *my* bed?"

Blaine shot Donovan a glance, curious what Ralph was saying on the other end of the line. Whatever it was, it wasn't good. Donovan was working his jaw, the muscle in his jaw clenching.

What happened to Mr. Cool?

"Plain. Wooden." Donovan worked his bottom lip. "What?" He glared at the ceiling. "You took it to the *garbage dump?* Who in the hell gave you permission to take my bed to a garbage dump?"

Mr. Cool went bye-bye.

Blaine decided to follow suit. Leave this fantasy world and reenter reality. Time for her to scoot back to work, call Ralph, and beg him to redeliver the brass bed to her sister because there was no way Blaine could return to Donovan's lair. Time to be practical, in control again and forget whatever crazy thoughts had temporarily turned her brain to love mush.

Speaking of reality, she desperately needed to take more allergy medicine. And just as doctors warned patients not to mix medicine with other substances, Blaine mixing her allergy medicine with a certain Donovan Roy was a dangerous combination.

As Donovan bunched his fist, letting Ralph know exactly where he could put his next delivery, Blaine slipped out the door.

"HELLO, STRANGER!" THE older man tossed something into the trash can under his desk.

Blaine, on her way to her desk, paused. "Dad, was that the crackle of a potato chip bag?"

He blinked, smiled, then nodded sheepishly.

"Thought you were on a diet." Good thing she'd popped that allergy pill after leaving Donovan's. She could talk and be understood again.

She sat down on her high-back desk chair, an ergonomic wonder she'd splurged on several years ago when business was better. She glanced out the office window at the sunlight streaming through the window, highlighting the white letters that spelled out The Blaine Saunders Temporary Agency.

Her dad brushed some crumbs off his mouth. "You're one to talk, Ms. Fast Food."

"I have a high metabolism."

"Just like your mama," he muttered under his breath. "I swear, you two could have been professional athletes if you'd put your minds to it."

Blaine smiled. She'd always excelled in sports. How many times as a kid had she fantasized about winning an Olympic gold medal? She could never decide for which event—at the rate her life was going lately, it'd be the bed-chasing event.

"I thought if I ate one more carrot, I'd turn into a bunny," her dad said, looking glum.

"But the doctor said—"

"Yes, I know, I need to lose twenty pounds."

"Thirty."

"I knew I should never have sent you to school. Now you know how to count."

Blaine smiled. "Any calls?"

"Just your sister. Something about a bed not showing up. I told her I hadn't heard about this bed..." He left the sentence hanging, waiting for Blaine to pick up the thread.

No way was Blaine falling for *that* old ruse. If she started talking about the bed, her father would start putting two and two together, and she was having a tough enough time dealing with her wanton one-nighter without her father knowing about it, too.

She started rifling through the sticky notes plastered around her desk. "Yeah, I need to follow up on that." Just which sticky had Ralph's number?

"Looking for something?" Her dad had ambled over to her desk, which sat a few feet from his.

"I need a sticky-note organizer," she muttered, picking up a white square and reading scribbled directions to someplace.

"Never understood why you have a computer if you keep writing on those things."

"Sometimes the old ways are the better ways."

"Roger that." Her father picked up a framed photo off Blaine's desk.

She glanced up. Her father was gazing at the picture of their family from years ago. She loved that picture, too. Her dad and mom looking young, happy. Her baby sister, Sonja, three years old, perched on her mother's lap. A nine-year-old Blaine standing next to her mom, grinning despite a gap where a front tooth used to be.

"Wish Mom could have been here to see Sonja get married."

He nodded, his gaze lingering on the photo. "Margaret," he whispered to the photo, "you woulda been proud." He set down the frame, careful to not disrupt a miniature NASCAR model car surrounded by an assortment of glass figurines that had belonged to his wife, now bequeathed to Blaine.

He cleared his throat. "Sonja also said she stayed awake until two this morning, waiting for that bed."

"I, uh, ran into a problem." *Named Donovan Roy.*

"Henry said you still have his truck."

She knew what her dad was doing. Fishing. He hated to not be in the know, hear what was happening in her life. Ever since he retired five years ago, this man had become a regular gossip hound.

She'd give him a project. That typically got the hound off the scent. "Would you be a sweetie, Dad, and call Henry? Tell him I might need to borrow his truck a bit longer, if that's okay. Maybe you and he can make lunch plans or something, too." *Maybe you can get out of the office and stop asking me questions about that bed.*

"Roger," her dad said, speaking in that new tone of voice he'd developed ever since she asked him to help out with the phones. After a lifetime of selling tires, who'd have thought this man would delight in a second career as a receptionist?

He walked back to his desk, sat down, and began dialing.

She continued sorting through the sticky notes while her dad left a message for Henry. After he hung up, he sighed with satisfaction. "Mission accomplished."

"Nice job."

"What happened to your clothes?"

"Huh?" She looked up.

Her father was pointing at the neckline of her T-shirt. "There's a tag hanging out. Is your shirt on backward?"

She looked down. Damn. She'd put her top on inside out. Why hadn't Donovan said anything? "I, uh, fell asleep trying to dismantle the bed."

Her father scooted forward a little in his chair. "Were you with David?"

She shot him an exasperated look. "No."

"Not David?"

"Not David," she said emphatically. "Dad..." She had to tread carefully here. "David and I broke up."

Her father's face went slack. "Broke up?" he repeated, his voice cracking.

Oh, no. Now she'd done it. "Dad, it's okay."

He grabbed a tissue from a box off his desk and dabbed at his eyes. "No, it's not."

She stood and crossed the few feet to where he sat. Standing next to him, she patted his arm, trying to figure out how to stop him from sliding into the "I want you to get married" speech.

"I want you to get married."

Too late. "I know."

"Your father isn't getting any younger, you know."

"No, you aren't," she said, not sure what she meant, but needing to say something.

"David seemed like such a nice boy."

"He's marrying someone else, Dad."

Her father gasped loudly. Rearing back, he flashed an alarmed look at Blaine. "No!"

"Yes."

"When he could have had the pick of the lot?"

Trust her father to see Blaine in a nobler light. "Well, guess he was on another lot because he picked someone else."

Her father thumped his desk with his fist. His bowling tournament award—a Plexiglas bowling pin on a stand—rattled. "The bastard!"

"Yes, that's more along the lines of how I was viewing him, too." Blaine smiled at her dad and headed back to her desk.

"So, if you weren't with David...?"

Blaine sat down. "There's no man involved." Well, that was sort of true if one leaned heavily on the word "involved." After all, a toss in the sack could hardly be construed as "involved."

"No man?"

"Dad," Blaine turned to face him squarely. "We've discussed this before. I don't need a man to be complete."

Her father opened both arms, gesturing broadly. "Who's talking complete? I just don't want you to be alone."

"I'm not alone. I have you. And Sonja. And soon a new brother-in-law."

Her father clasped his hands together. "And I wanted David to be your date at your sister's wedding. It's not right that the maid of honor is dateless." He had that faraway look in his eye again. Blaine made a mental note to slip some *Field and Stream* magazines into his stash of *Good Housekeeping*.

She spied a pink square of paper with Ralph's name and number. "Bingo! Found it!" She quickly picked up the phone and dialed. After what seemed a gazillion rings, a man finally answered.

"Hullo?"

"Ralph?"

"Yeah?"

"This is Blaine Saunders. You delivered a brass bed yesterday to Circle Drive—"

"Look," Ralph cut in, "that dude already called. Somebody needs to tell him to take time to smell the roses."

"Yes, he's, uh, a bit stressed, losing his bed..." Blaine cleared her throat. This next part wasn't going to be easy. "I was wondering," she said, forcing herself to sound oozy sweet, the way Sonja sounded when she was buttering up some guy, "if you could pick up that brass bed and redeliver it—"

"Hey," Ralph cut in again, "it's already being redelivered at no charge, just like that dude wanted."

Redelivered? "Uh, he doesn't know where to deliver the bed."

"Well he found out 'cause he gave me very explicit instructions."

"Yeah?" Sheesh, she was starting to sound like Ralph. "Where?"

"The Blazing Saddles Motel."

"What?" Blaine shot out of her seat, still gripping the receiver to her ear. "You can't deliver the bed there! That's a...a..." *smarmy, slimey, sex motel*.

"Well, I *did* deliver the bed there—Barry is driving it out there even as we speak—"

"I want you to stop him and deliver it someplace else!" So much for oozy sweet. Most of Manitou Springs probably heard that little outburst.

"No!" Ralph muttered an expletive. "You know," he said, tightly, "until that brass bed came into my life, I had an easygoing, happy little delivery business."

The phone clicked off.

Blaine stood there, still gripping the receiver, unable to fathom what had just happened.

"Blaine, honey, what is it?" her father asked.

"Sonja's wedding gift is on the verge of becoming..." Images of people in leather, wielding whips, doing unthinkable things on Sonja's wedding-gift bed zapped through Blaine's mind.

She slammed down the phone. "I must go to the Blazing Saddles Motel."

"That...that...*sex* motel?" Now her father was standing. "I know I've been pushing you to find a guy, but—"

"Dad, this isn't about me! This is about Sonja's bed!" Blaine checked the wall clock. Almost one. If she hopped on it, maybe she'd arrive at the motel before the bed did.

She grabbed the keys to Henry's truck. "I gotta go. Hold down the fort."

"Don't drive like one of those NASCAR drivers, you hear?"

Her love of speed and cars started when she saw Tom Cruise in *Days of Thunder*. After that, she started watching NASCAR races on TV, imagining herself ripping loose in one of those souped-up cars. "Like Henry's truck can even hit fifty miles an hour."

Her father frowned. "How'd Sonja's bed end up at the Blazing Saddles?"

"Some idiot had it delivered there." She started heading for the door. "Whatever you do, don't tell Sonja," she yelled over her shoulder. Blaine could hear it now. *The bride wore white, the bed wore red.*

Blaine groaned as she pushed open the door, inhaling the world of pollen.

4

DONOVAN RINSED THE PLATE, scraping off the last remnants of huevos rancheros, the eggs and chili sitting warm in his belly. Now that his stomach was satisfied, his mind could reflect on the door shutting behind his surprise guest an hour ago.

Maybe she'd left so abruptly because he yelled. Well, the conversation with Ralph hadn't been going well at that point, that was for sure. But Donovan needed to watch his flashpoint. Which, unfortunately, flashed more quickly when he was tired, worn down. Old behaviors die hard.

Took him years, and a good therapist, to get a handle on his anger. And to realize his outbursts were rooted in his home life growing up.

Back then his home was a comfortable many-acred ranch outside Manitou Springs. A place where they raised some cattle, horses, even a few chickens. Outside, Donovan and his three brothers were constantly busting to take care of the animals, mend fences and corrals, repair machinery. Outside, they toiled and laughed and cursed if their mother wasn't within earshot.

But everyone changed as soon as they went indoors.

Inside, they grew quiet, kept to themselves. It took him years to understand why.

Nobody talked about real issues. About what was going on inside their minds, their heads, their hearts.

His mom—her face tight, unsmiling—was continuously cleaning, cooking, her interactions with her sons mostly terse reminders to pick up their clothes, put away their dishes, don't drink out of the milk container.

His dad was a salesman who'd married a rancher's daughter who inherited the family ranch. With four sons, his dad was content to let *them* learn the ranching game. He liked to joke that it was time to *go* to bed, not get up, when the rooster crows. Unlike his uptight mother, his dad was gregarious, boastful and the one the boys turned to when they wanted to borrow money or the car.

No one discussed the undercurrent in the house, a nearly audible static. It was as though the energy in the house had been strung so tight, if anyone dared to acknowledge it, it would snap and explode in their faces.

So they went about their lives, faking that everything was all right, nothing was wrong.

Except his mom. She didn't pretend. She repressed.

Of all the brothers, only Donovan knew why. He hadn't meant to know, nor did his parents want him to know, but he'd accidentally overheard them talking when he was fourteen. The long year he was bedridden, thanks to a crushed femur—and other complications—after his horse had fallen on him.

Lying on the rented hospital bed in his room, his

world shrunken to what he could see outside his window, one day he'd heard whispering in the hallway. The hushed words grew louder, the current breaking, and the crackle of truth reached his ears.

"Not another get-rich scheme," his mother had suddenly cried. "We don't even have enough to pay for groceries, and you spent your paycheck on *that?*"

"Shut up, Karen." Donovan hadn't even recognized his father's voice at first. The jovial tone had turned venomous, cruel.

And then the voices diminished, the static returning.

And that's when Donovan understood why the gas and electricity had been turned off twice that year. Why he'd find his mother up late, alone in the kitchen, scribbling numbers on a notepad.

His father, with his bottomless pocketful of dreams, had plunged the family into debt.

Being bedridden, Donovan had had ample time that year to tune into that silent interior world he retreated to more and more. There, he'd contemplated things like truth and family and money.

Especially money.

He'd eventually decided that it in itself wasn't the root of all evil...what was evil was the abuse of it.

After his recovery, while his parents continued to put on a brave front, acting as though nothing was wrong, Donovan started shoplifting, stealing, fighting.

The shoplifting stopped when he got caught stealing a dirt bike and, thanks to an agreement between his parents and the store owner, no charges were pressed if Donovan paid for the bike. It cost him his entire summer earnings, plus a year's free labor every Saturday at the store.

The fistfights took longer to stop. If a boy tossed an insult, Donovan tossed a fist. At twenty-four, after ending up in a jail after a bar brawl, a judge gave Donovan a choice. Jail or therapy. Grudgingly, he took the latter.

And so began the long process of Donovan learning that his thefts and temper were just tools he'd adopted to cope with the "secret" at home.

And, learning that, he took the next steps to understand how to control his rage. He wasn't always successful, but he sure as hell knew how to count to ten.

More often, though, he'd retreat, reassess the situation, then plan how to diplomatically resolve the issue. And when he retreated, it was typically to his home, his sanctuary. A place, like that still place in his mind, that was unencumbered with others.

Except for last night.

Donovan headed back into the living room, swearing he still caught her scent—that teasing smell of almonds.

He glanced into his empty bedroom. After an intense verbal exchange, during which Donovan fought hard to return to a "cooler" state, Ralph had finally backed down and had one of his buddies pick up the brass bed. Donovan hadn't known the woman's home address, where obviously the bed belonged, so he'd asked for it to be delivered to her business.

Only after the bed was gone did Donovan think about how awkward it could be if a big brass bed was delivered to her while she was in a meeting, or interviewing a prospective client.

Donovan might be a moody cuss, but he wasn't vindictive. And she'd probably think the latter if he didn't explain to her that when Ralph suddenly caved in and agreed to redeliver the bed, Donovan didn't want to lose the advantage.

So he'd quickly thrown out the only destination he knew. The Blaze Sauddles Agency.

Ralph had repeated the word "Blaze," emitted a low whistle, then chuckled while saying, "Okee, don't need no address for that!" Manitou was so small, Ralph probably knew most businesses' addresses.

And now the bed is being delivered to her agency, and she's going to think I'm one vindictive sonofa—

He headed to the phone. He'd call, explain why he had it delivered there. Hell, he'd even admit that he'd fixed his old bed so many times this past year, he was ready to take the damn thing to the garbage dump himself.

He punched in the number for Information.

"What city?" asked the pleasant electronic voice.

"Manitou Springs."

"Name?"

"Blaze Sauddles Agency."

There was a long pause, a click, then a real voice spoke.

"I don't have a listing for a Blaze Sauddles Agency."

Donovan paused. "No, I'm certain it's Blaze...Blaze something."

"Blazing Saddles?"

That raunchy X-rated motel outside town? "Hell, no," he blurted. "It's an agency." What had she called it? "A temporary agency."

"Let me check." After a moment, the operator said, "I have a Blaine Saunders Temporary Agency on Ruxton."

Blaine Saunders? Boy, those allergies did mean tricks with her sinuses. "Yeah, that's the one."

After dialing, the phone rang twice before a male voice answered in a pleasant, but authoritative, tone. "Welcome. This is the Blaine Saunders Agency. May I be of service?"

"I'd like to speak to Blaine Saunders. Please."

There was a moment of silence, during which Donovan swore he heard the man gasp. "I'm sure she'd be delighted to speak with you, but unfortunately she's not here at the moment..."

"Do you know when she'll be back?"

"No, but...maybe I can help you? What's your name?"

The man's authoritative tone had been replaced by a rather enthusiastic one. "Uh, Donovan."

"Donovan," the man repeated slowly. "Never heard of you, son. Last name?"

Never heard of you? "Roy."

"Donovan Roy. Sounds strong, loyal. You employed?"

At first Donovan was thrown off, but after all, this was a temporary employment agency. "Yes, but—"

"What do you do for a living?"

As his therapist had often counseled Donovan in the

past, sometimes it was better to go with the flow than to fight it. *Think about water flowing around a rock.* "I have my own consulting business, but really I called to speak with Blaine about something else—"

"What kind of consulting?"

Go with the flow. Go with the flow. "Computers."

"Oh, could Blaine ever use your help. She's addicted to sticky notes."

But sometimes, if the flow took a weird turn, it was okay to take a detour. "Hey, I'll call back later—"

"Wait a minute. You married?"

Donovan sank down into his kitchen chair. Ever since he got back from his most recent business trip, it was as though he'd not returned home. It was more like he'd stepped into an alternate universe.

"What does my being married have to do with anything?"

"Uh, office procedure."

"To ask people their marital status? I believe that's against the law."

"Oh." The man cleared his throat. "Well, can I take a message for Blaine?"

Considering this man's penchant for questions, Donovan thought it prudent to simply leave his number. "Yes, please tell her I called." He gave his name and number, then paused. He should probably ask if a big, brass bed had been delivered, but just as he started to speak, the man started talking again.

"She should be back later this afternoon."

Donovan glanced at his redwood clock. Nearly two o'clock. Not such a big surprise considering they'd slept till noon, then talked for thirty minutes. Throw in that exhilarating discussion with Ralph, and the huevos rancheros, and no wonder it was almost midafternoon.

But "later this afternoon" could still be hours away. And he couldn't wait hours to talk to Blaine.

One of the pluses about small-town Manitou Springs was that it was a cinch to locate someone on the spur of the moment. Yeah, that would be much better. He'd track her down. Explain face-to-face why the bed was delivered to her business before she returned to her agency and got a big surprise.

"Would you mind telling me where she is?" Donovan asked.

"Yes," the man said tersely. "At the Blazing Saddles Motel."

"*What?*"

"Yeah, can you believe it?" The man snorted. "That's where some *idiot* had her bed delivered."

MINUTES LATER, DONOVAN was on the phone with the Blazing Saddles Motel. Some gentleman with a twangy accent had answered.

"I believe you have my bed," Donovan began.

"Uh-huh. You lookin' to make a reservation?"

"No, no. I mean, my bed—well, actually someone else's bed—was delivered to your establishment by mistake."

"Someone *else's* bed."

"That's correct."

"Uh-huh."

Donovan heard a TV in the background, which obviously accounted for the man's annoying lack of concentration on this discussion.

"So," Donovan continued, "Since the wrong bed was delivered to your establishment, I'll make arrangements to have it picked up."

"Picked up."

"That's correct."

"Ain't got no pickups here. Against the law."

He eased in a slow, calming breath. "I'm not talking about pickups. I'm talking about you having the wrong bed."

"The wrong bed."

"Yes!" Donovan pinched the bridge of his nose, reminding himself to go with the flow.

"Uh-huh. You want to make a reservation?"

"No!"

Click.

Donovan stared at the phone. "An X-rated motel just hung up on me!"

He started to punch the recall button, then stopped. It'd only be a series of "uh-huh" and "Do you want to make a reservation?" again.

He hung up the receiver, thinking through his next steps. Or non-steps. He could forget all about the brass bed being at the Blazing Saddles. Forget that Blaine Saunders was on her way to retrieve the bed...

"Yeah, right," he muttered. "And what if she takes too much of her allergy medicine again, and..." He imagined her pink, curvy body naked, sprawled across that big brass bed...which was now sitting in some sleazy room at the Blazing Saddles Motel. He could just see some guy checking in, seeing that lovely body, and thinking this was better than a mint on the pillow.

"No way in hell," Donovan muttered, feeling a jolt of red-hot possessiveness. He needed to protect her.

He grabbed his car keys off the kitchen table and headed out the front door.

"LOOK," SAID THE GUY behind the Blazing Saddles registration desk, a cheap contraption that looked like glued-together wood paneling. "The owner's on vacation. Until he gets back, the bed stays here."

Donovan was grinding his teeth so hard, he was surprised one of them hadn't chipped by now. It didn't help that a small TV behind the desk was on some station with wobbly images and static sound.

The static reminded him of home. Reminded him to speak his truth.

"That bed doesn't belong to you," Donovan said tightly, forcing himself to sound calm. He'd looked around for Blaine when he arrived here ten minutes ago, but so far she hadn't arrived so Donovan had taken matters into his own hands.

"So you've said," the guy said wearily. "About twenty times."

Donovan forced himself to maintain eye contact with the weasel's little black pupils. "It belongs to the Blaine Saunders Agency. Call the number. It's listed. They'll verify that the bed belongs to them."

The guy shifted a toothpick from one side of his

mouth to the other. "Uh-huh. And then I'll call my cousin Irene who'll say it belongs to her, too."

"Cousin Irene?" *Go with the flow. Go with the flow.*

"But unlike Irene," Donovan countered, "Blaine Saunders will have a receipt."

The man leaned forward. "I don't care if she has a dozen receipts. The owner has been renovating several rooms, and when something arrives, I sign for it and tell 'em where to put it. I ain't having the owner come back and find I'm also *giving* stuff away, just 'cause some hot-to-trot fellow claims it's his."

"Blaine's."

"Whoever's."

They stared at each other so long, Donovan felt his eye twitch. "How about I just check the room, so I can confirm it's the bed I'm looking for?"

"How's about you take a long walk off a short—"

"How's about *you* take a—" Donovan was leaning forward so far, he could smell the stench of cigarette smoke in the man's clothes. *Don't say it. Don't go there.*

He leaned back. "How's about I apologize," he said, mustering every ounce of civility he had, "for our getting off on the wrong foot."

Man, his therapist would be proud. Donovan Roy practicing the art of cool in a heated moment.

He forced a smile. "Let me rephrase my question. May I, please, check the room to ensure the bed is here?" He'd figure out what to do about retrieving the bed after that.

"You can check *into* a room, but not check one."

Obstinate sonofa— "Which room has the brass bed?"

"Don't know if it's a brass or not, but some new bed was delivered today to the Parisian Fantasy room. Only bed delivery we've had these past few days."

Parisian Fantasy? In some X-rated, bohunk, cowboy-titled motel? Donovan pulled out his wallet. Maybe he could slip this in as part of his recent business trip, make it a write-off. *Nix that. One look at the motel name, and my accountant will laugh his head off.*

It wasn't that Donovan didn't make enough money to afford such expenditures. Actually, he made fantastic money at his consulting business. But the bulk of his money went to fixing the past. Paying off the voluminous debts his father had accrued over the years. Ensuring his mom was able to keep a portion of the ranch, although she insisted on selling those damn eggs, which still ticked Donovan. Not at his mother's decision, but at his father who left her life in such a mess.

Maybe in the past he hadn't helped his mother before things damn near crashed and burned, but he could help another woman now. Plus, it was his fault he'd had the bed delivered to this place. He owed it to Blaine to make things right.

Donovan handed the card to the man. "I'd like to reserve the Parisian Fantasy room."

BLAINE SAT ON THE SIDE of the road, miles from anywhere, in Henry's pickup. She stared through the bug-splattered windshield at the steam roiling and hissing from under the hood.

"Wish I hadn't cancelled my cell phone," she muttered to herself, opening the door and jumping onto the dusty shoulder of the road. A few months ago, canceling the cell had seemed the smart thing to do. Another way to cut her expenses.

She hadn't expected to be stuck miles outside of town with no way to contact anyone.

Blaine blew a strand of hair out of her eyes and stared at the pickup. "Henry will never let me borrow you again." And rightfully so. Keeping his truck longer than originally agreed upon, then having it blow up, would hardly endear her to her dad's old friend.

Blaine looked at the dark clouds that cloaked the top of Pikes Peak. "Wonderful. Another afternoon storm's brewing." Although everyone in the region was accustomed to sudden storms year around, they were especially potent during the early summer.

She checked her wristwatch. Almost three. She looked down the two-lane blacktop, guessing she was four, five miles from the Blazing Saddles Motel. *If I walk fast, I can probably make it there before the rain starts. At the motel, I'll borrow a phone and call Dad about the truck. He and Henry are best buds—they'll figure out something. And I'll write an IOU to Henry for a free "fix it" at his house.*

That lifted her mood a bit. Maybe she'd inconvenienced Henry, but she'd make it up to him. *And then I'll brainstorm with Dad how we can get the bed redelivered.*

Over an hour later, Blaine trudged along the asphalt road, praying that the flashing red neon sign she'd spied in the distance was the Blazing Saddles Motel. Her legs ached. Her hair, soaked with perspiration, clung to her face and neck. The storm clouds were moving in, shading the sky a dull pewter. She could smell the ozone in the air, sense the threat of the impending storm.

Ten minutes later, she was close enough to see a saddle outlined in flashing red neon. Underneath it were the words "Blazing Saddles" followed by a list of amenities. Hot tub in each room, free coffee.

Free coffee? Blaine swallowed, hard. It'd been such a crazy day, she hadn't had time to eat. All she'd had was coffee at Donovan's. As her mom had always said, Blaine's doggedness was her greatest strength and her greatest weakness. Sure, she got things done, but she often forgot to take care of other things. Like herself.

She stepped into the registration lobby, a room that contained the ugliest, fake-wood desk she'd ever seen, a rack of magazines and two folding chairs. Blaine released a breath of relief at the onslaught of chilled air-conditioning. Then she caught her reflection in the glass. Her jeans and inside-out T-shirt were wrinkled and smudged with dirt and sweat. And thanks to the wind and dust, her normally limp hair now stuck out all over.

I look like a deranged roadrunner.

She patted down her hair—wishing for the first time in her life that she carted around girly things like combs and lipstick. Her finger absently tugged on an earlobe. She frowned, checking the other earlobe with its dangling earring of stars.

Great. Somewhere on my cross-country trek to Smarm Motel, I lost one of my favorite pair of earrings.

She slapped the silver bell on the desk.

Ding ding ding.

A man dressed in a blue-and-white checkered cowboy shirt ambled out to the desk. "Howdy," he said, looking her up and down.

She smiled, trying to act as though she looked normal. "Hi," she said with as much confidence as her dirt-caked throat would allow. "I'm looking for a bed."

He raised both bushy eyebrows. "Not again," he muttered before asking, "Brass bed?"

"Yes!" Thank God, something was going right today.

The guy gave his head a weary shake. "Them must be popular this afternoon. Someone else asked for it about an hour ago."

"They did?" Images of whips and chains on her sister's wedding-gift bed flashed through her mind. "You didn't give it to them, did you?"

The man blinked. "Yep. But if it's an interesting bed you want…" He opened up the registration book. "We got some other fancy types. Wild West room's got a bed made of antlers, Hollywood Haven has one that looks like a casting couch—"

"No! No!" She clutched the edge of the faux wood desk. "I *need* the brass bed! It's *my* bed. I have a receipt!" She dug into her pocket and waved her tissue at him. Fighting the urge to curse, she dug into her pocket again. "Well, I had it earlier..." She thought back. Last she recalled, she'd flashed it to Milly. Maybe it was lying outside Donovan's apartment. "Let me borrow your phone—I can call someone who'll verify the receipt exists."

He stared at her for a long moment, the only sound the faint rattle of the air-conditioning. "Sorry," he said calmly. "No phone privileges for noncustomers. And if you ain't gettin' a room, I'm gonna have to ask you to leave."

She stared at him, feeling the sting of tears at the corners of her eyes. Damn damn damn. Some pervert—or perverts—was doing unmentionable things on her sister's wedding gift. Blaine swallowed, hard, knowing she'd lost any last shred of dignity, but needing to forge on anyway. "Maybe the people who checked into the room with the brass bed would be willing to move into the Wild West room instead?"

"I'm gonna have to ask you to—"

"Why not?" she squeaked. "Brass beds are a dime a dozen, but *antlers!* Now *that's* a bed! The possibilities are endless." Damn, she had no idea what she was even talking about anymore. In her mind's eye, all she could see was the magical brass bed...and she'd say anything, anything to get her hands on it again.

The guy was looking uneasy. "Look, I'm only filling in for the owner. I don't want trouble. The guy wanted a brass bed, so he got the brass bed. If you want one of the other rooms, fine. Otherwise, please leave or I'll have to call the sheriff."

But all Blaine heard was "the guy." So some guy had

specifically asked for the brass bed. Maybe things weren't too bad. After all, what kind of damage could a single guy do to a single bed?

Time to think creatively.

"Yes, those other rooms did sound interesting," she said, forcing herself to sound like maybe, just maybe, she might check into a room after all. She cleared her throat and plastered on a smile. "Let me think...what other room might I like..."

Pretending to be lost in room contemplation, she shifted her gaze to the window that looked out onto the parking lot. She gasped and pointed. "Oh my God. Somebody's breaking into that Chevy Impala!" She shot a wide-eyed look at the man behind the desk. "If someone breaks into a car while it's on your property, are you liable for the damages?"

Yelling an expletive, the guy bolted out the door.

And in those few moments before he realized no one was breaking into anything, she glanced at the registration book. Funny, everyone was named Smith or Jones...

Except for room number six, where a Mr. Donovan Roy had signed in.

Donovan was *here*?

She frowned. It hadn't made sense that he'd had the bed delivered here. She'd assumed it was some kind of vindication for her accidentally losing his bed.

But he was here, and had asked for the room with the brass bed?

Just then the door burst open. "You sure somebody

was breaking into the Impala?" the motel man said, heaving breaths.

She looked outside, then put on her best surprised look. "Oh, he must have gotten away." She smiled and batted her eyes, the way she'd seen Sonja do a thousand times. "You know, I've thought about those beds, but nothing jingles my bell if you get my drift. I'll just be leaving now."

And she casually walked past him into the outdoors. Gusts of wind tousled her hair as she walked toward the cars, hoping the guy would think she was heading to hers.

She sneezed. *Thank God it's going to rain soon.* A good rain cleansed the air, made breathing easier. She peeked over her shoulder. Through the glass wall of the lobby, no one stood behind the registration desk.

Good!

With a flying leap, she jumped behind a pickup truck and peeked around its dented bumper, searched the singular row of doors for the one marked six.

Fortunately, it was the last room at the end of the L-shaped motel.

After a last glance at the lobby to ensure it was empty, she made a mad dash for door number six just as a drop of rain splatted against her head.

Reaching the door, she rapped sharply.

The door opened. There stood Donovan, still dressed in that donut T-shirt and ripped jeans. The sight of his rugged, tan face sent a surprise shiver through Blaine.

"You're here!" he exclaimed, stepping back. "I was getting worried about you."

Worried? Over her? "You got the bed?" she asked, pushing past him.

The room was so dark, she had to stop after a few steps. She squinted, trying to decipher shapes in the shadows punctured by red lights. "What is this? A dark room?"

"Uh, no," Donovan chuckled. "It's the Parisian Fantasy room. Give yourself a few minutes—your eyes will adjust."

She squeezed her eyes shut to help the adjusting process along. When she reopened them, objects had taken shape in the red-tinged room. Not crystal clear, but enough to decipher what's what. Her gaze traveled around the room, finally landing on a glint of curved metal.

"The bed...!" she exclaimed, feeling giddy. It was saved, it was hers, it...

"It's not my bed," she whispered hoarsely, her heart plummeting. She looked at Donovan. "What'd you do with my bed?"

5

"I DIDN'T DO ANYTHING with your bed," Donovan said. "Except request it be delivered to your job—"

"Job?" She held open her hands. "Do I look like some kind of bordello babe?"

There was a long pause. "Uh, it's dark in here," Donovan finally muttered. "I can't really see you all that well."

"I'm dressed in dirt-caked jeans," she shot back, "an inside-out T-shirt that reads NASCAR Roars on its front when I've had the opportunity to get dressed *properly*, a pair of sneakers that have lost their tread and one earring."

"One?"

She ignored his question, not wanting to digress into how she'd lost one of her earrings during today's insane walkathon to this sex oasis. It had probably happened when she'd pulled back her hair to cool her hot, sweaty neck.

And those had been one of her fav pair of earrings, too. A birthday gift from her dad. They'd had little dangling silver stars "to remind you of your dreams" he'd said. She pulled off the remaining earring and stuck it in her jeans pocket. Didn't want to lose the last one, too.

"I know you don't work here." Donovan's voice drew her back to their discussion.

"Sorry. It's just that lately I feel I'm either losing, or on the verge of losing, so much in my life. And that bed's become..." She stopped herself, feeling silly describing how a brass bed had become something extraordinary. But in her heart, it had become far more than a bed. It was an enchanted object, capable of transforming life from the ordinary to the magical.

She sniffed, fighting the urge to cry.

That was another thing that irked her lately. Blaine never had roller-coaster emotions the way other women did. *Never.* At school dances, when other girls clustered in the bathroom to slather on lipstick and squeal over boys, Blaine had hung out behind the gymnasium, sneaking a cigarette or playing cards with the geeky boys who felt as uncomfortable as she did at those frilly school functions. But her dad had made her go—after losing her mom, he was determined to help Blaine do the girl stuff.

And later, after high school, when it seemed the same girls were squealing over each other's engagement rings and wedding dresses, Blaine remained focused on doing well in her accounting classes because she was determined to open her own business. The only time she squealed was when she earned an A in calculus.

She had grown so accustomed to being responsible and in control, that for her to feel the roller-coaster emotions that she had in the last few days was downright scary. Blaine's solid, upright world was on a tilt.

She dug her toe into the thick rug, suppressing the urge to just kick the hell out of it.

"You okay?" Donovan asked.

"Yes," she said tightly.

"Maybe I should explain why Ralph thought the bed was supposed to be delivered here?"

She snorted.

"I'll take that to be a yes."

The man was unnervingly collected. Was this the same guy who had raged at Ralph earlier?

"This morning," Donovan began, "I thought you said your name was 'Blaze' something—"

"*Blaze?*"

"Well, that's how it sounded when you spoke."

"Because I was congested," she clarified.

"Yes, *exactly*, so it was easy to misunderstand things you said. So, I told Ralph to deliver the bed to Blaze-something's business, and he *swore* he knew exactly where it was."

"He swore?"

"Actually, he whistled."

Nobody ever whistled at Blaine—hell, even *she* didn't know how to whistle. But the rest she understood. She'd been so clogged up this morning, it was a miracle Donovan could decipher anything she said. And considering he was here, when he could have blown off her bed problem, the guy was A-OK. A real gent.

"Thanks," she said softly, "for being here...and for thinking I could really have a name like 'Blaze.' Makes me sound far more exotic than I really am, like a stripper or something."

She could sense his smile. She smiled too, feeling better that they'd cleared the air.

"You must have taken an allergy pill today," Donovan commented. "You sound pretty good."

"Took one earlier," she affirmed. "Plus there weren't as many pollens out here, fortunately, or my trek to the motel would have been a disaster."

"Trek?"

"My dad's friend's truck broke down. That's why I'm so sweaty and dusty—I walked the rest of the way. Took me a while." Sheesh, she didn't want to sound like a pity party. "But I can handle it. Spent years playing sports."

"You're a trouper, Blaine. I admire that."

He said it as though she were the most awesome woman on the planet. She was so taken aback at the surprise compliment, she couldn't think of anything to say, so she just stared back at him.

Faint red light glazed his dark form, but she could still see the solid bulk of his shoulders, the outline of those taut, muscled hips she remembered too well from when he stood naked in front of her this morning. Add the room's crimson hues, and his cool-blue attitude, and it was all she could do to stand here, remembering to breathe.

Overhead, a ceiling fan spun in circles, its rhythmic sound competing with the beating of her heart.

In a crazy rush of feeling, she wished she had better memories of last night. As it was, it felt like a dream, still making her question if it had really happened. Wouldn't it be something to have those memories indelibly burned into her brain, like a red-hot secret she could retrieve and remember again and again...

And what she'd remember would be as magical as her bed. Because now she realized how it and Donovan were intertwined, both curled provocatively together in her fantasies. Just as one sparked her libido, so did the other.

As they stood in the muted shadows, two crimson-gilded forms staring each other down, she caught his scent. That mind-reeling tang of musk and male.

A hot ache raced through her, careening wildly as though speeding to the finish line, and she wondered what was at the end of the road for her and Donovan. Maybe they were more than last night...maybe he felt the same attraction she felt...

Get real. My clothes are dusty, clinging to my body. And thank God it's dark in here so he doesn't see my windblown, matted hairdo.

Oh, yeah, I'm the stud magnet of the century. Just the kind of gal a guy dreams he'll be stuck in a motel room with.

Sucking in a deep breath, Blaine made a great show of perusing the room. "Is there a phone in here?" she asked, forcing herself to sound level, together, as though not one teensy sizzling thought had just crossed her mind. "'Cause we should call Ralph, explain this new twist in the ongoing bed saga, and I also need to call my dad about the abandoned truck."

She squinted, trying to pick out anything that resembled a phone.

Behind her, in front of the draped window, was a high-backed love seat. In front of it, a low table that appeared to be glass and wrought iron. In the center of the room, the bed, its posts draped with some kind of filmy, see-through stuff. Next to the bed, a round table with what looked to be some little boxes on it. And on the far side of the bed, against the back corner of the room, there appeared to be some kind of oversized pedestal.

Pedestal?

Just what did people do at the Blazing Saddles Motel?

Fighting images of naked bodies dancing wildly on pedestals, Blaine quickly scanned the entire room again, mindlessly counting the number of lamps with red-glass fixtures. Had to be at least five, their combined light infusing the room with a hazy, hot glow.

She looked back at Donovan, admiring how that hazy, hot glow poured over him like molten heat. Damn, the man was lethal enough without coating him in a seductive light. Right now, he looked like a bigger, badder version of that hunky actor Matthew McConaughey.

"I looked for a phone after I checked in," said Donovan matter-of-factly, "but it appears these rooms don't have them."

He sounded so cool, so collected…good thing she'd reined in her primal urge a few moments ago.

"Probably afraid someone will call the Decorator Police," Blaine quipped.

He chuckled. She loved the sound. Deep, full of

mirth. "I tried using my cell..." He motioned to a small dark object on the glass table, "but it's out of roaming range. Can't get a signal."

"No room phone, no cell." Blaine's legs brushed something firm, plush. She glanced down. Appeared to be some kind of velvet-upholstered ottoman. Eager to give her body a rest, she lowered herself and sat on it.

"What about the lobby phone?" she asked. "I can't go back there. Long story. Don't ask. But *you* could call Ralph, ask where he delivered my bed, and this whole bed mystery will be solved!"

"Won't work. Ralph won't talk to me."

Disappointment knotted in her chest. "What're you talking about?"

"I already used the lobby phone. Ralph hung up as soon as I identified myself. Trust me, after our morning's negotiations to redeliver the bed, that man doesn't want to deal with me again."

Blaine flashed on Ralph's comment that Donovan needed to take time to smell the roses. "I'd ask you to use the lobby phone to call my dad, but if he sees 'Blazing Saddles' on the caller ID, and realizes you and I are together, he'll go into serious matchmaker mode."

After a beat, Donovan asked, "Does your dad answer the phone at the agency?"

"Yes."

"We've already been matchmaked."

She sighed heavily. "The hound's on the hunt again. No, no, let's not have you phoning Dad again for the time being."

She settled back on the ottoman, looking at the big-shouldered, bigger-than-life silhouette of Donovan Roy. How tall was he? Six-two? Three?

But even though he was big and bad, he wasn't your average macho type, she thought. The kind of guy whose personality has the depth of a mud puddle. No, Donovan had more twists and turns than a rushing Colorado river. Calm and collected one moment, churning violently the next. And he might look rough, but she'd seen those books on his shelves—subjects ranging from biographies of Civil War generals to classic literature.

The man was complex. Rugged attire, refined mind.

The kind of man she wouldn't mind be matchmaked with.

"You're awfully quiet," Donovan suddenly said.

"Just...thinking."

"About what?"

"The...free coffee in the room," she lied.

He did that rough, husky chuckle again. "You're my kind of woman. Coffee. Never start a day without it. Hey, I'm tired of talking and not seeing your face." Donovan headed toward the window. "I tried to open those drapes earlier, but they're more fluff than substance. I'll give it another shot."

"Oh, you don't want to see me," Blaine said quickly, more than mildly panicked at the idea of her grungy self being more visible. "I'm all dusty, my clothes are wrinkled, and—"

"Pshaw." He moved through the shadows, his feet

brushing heavily across the thick rug. "Woman fret too much about their looks."

She heard the rustling of thick drapes. "Damn velvet..." He muttered a few more expletives. "Good. Here's a cord. I'll give it a pull..."

A stream of hazy light, almost a gray-blue, seeped through the parted drapes as Donovan tugged on a thick gold cord and tied it off.

No wonder the light was so muted. Through the foot-wide opening in the drapes, Blaine saw how the skies had grown darker, laden with rain clouds. In the distance, over the summit of Pikes Peak, several jagged flashes of yellow lightning ripped through the sky.

"See that?" asked Donovan.

"Yes."

He looked over his shoulder at Blaine. "Glad you got here in time."

"I didn't want to end up like Mrs. Skinner."

All the locals knew about Mrs. Skinner, a Texan who'd visited Pikes Peak in 1911 and insisted on climbing to the summit despite warnings of an impending summer storm.

"Doubt if you'd have been buried in snow like Mrs. Skinner. After all, her goal was the summit and yours was this motel."

"Yeah, but we're both bullheaded when we get a goal in mind."

"*That's* for sure." He whooped a laugh. "Anyone who walks miles in this godforsaken heat has more than her share of grit and determination."

Blaine grinned, liking Donovan's teasing. "Okay, I

'fess up to being bullheaded, but I also have enough common sense to respect the weather around here."

"Unlike Mrs. Skinner," Donovan mused, looking at the white crest of Pikes Peak in the distance.

"Guess they found the bodies only two miles from the summit," she said.

"They were holding hands."

"I'd never heard that." But now that she did, Blaine was more than impressed that Donovan recalled such a romantic detail in an otherwise tragic story. And if he had such a romantic streak, why didn't she see any signs of lady friends around his place?

He had loner written all over him, but Blaine had no doubt he had more than his fair share of women throwing themselves at him. And if her dreamy, hazy memories were correct, he was also one hell of a hot lover, so the guy had plenty of experience.

Thinking of her own experience with him, she turned to look at the brass bed, finally able to see it in the faint light from the window.

It was like expecting Santa Claus and finding some skinny guy in an ill-fitting red suit.

The metal looked dull, whereas her bed sparkled. And this bed had some loopy curls of metal, whereas her bed had sleek cylinders that coiled and curved with a grace that bordered on mystical.

She sighed deeply. "We should drive back to Manitou, hunt down Ralph—"

Her words were cut short by the distant crash of thunder, which rolled threateningly across the skies for several long moments. Rain splattered heavily against the window.

"Storm's getting closer, Mrs. Skinner. If we get caught in a flash flood, we can kiss not only the bed, but possibly our lives goodbye."

"You're right."

"I know."

She smiled. "You know, you have a wicked sense of humor when you let down your guard."

"What guard?" he said, feigning defensiveness.

"If you keep up this charming act, I'm going to like you for more than your body," she blurted. Damn, damn, damn. And she had been pretty darn good at thinking before speaking for the last, oh, few minutes.

She slid a glance at Donovan. Even in the hazy light, she caught his very amused look.

"Well, now," he said, "I'll just have to put a lid on the charm, won't I?"

His husky, teasing tone made her skin prickle with anticipation. She wanted to toss off a quick retort, something sassy to one-up him, but her mind had gone on strike.

Oh, there were a few words that popped into her mind. Things like "Bite me!" "Touch me!" She bit her tongue to prevent any slips of it and sat stiffly on the ottoman, gripping its sides as though it were some kind of life raft.

"You're worrying me," he finally said. "You've stopped talking."

She nodded, afraid to open her mouth.

Donovan crossed the room and stood in front of her.

He had the disadvantage of facing the light streaming through the window, but he could still see she had one hell of a wary look in her eyes.

But there was something he saw in those eyes. Something soft, vulnerable that gave his heart a squeeze.

She was...special.

Irritating as hell sometimes, no doubt bullheaded enough to play tackle on the Broncos *without* a helmet, but...special.

Maybe because he'd never been with a woman who felt like his equal. The way she pursued her goals—like that bed—reminded him of himself. Someone with that kind of tenacity grabbed life with both hands and rode it, hard, to get what she wanted. Although he didn't "get" this whole brass bed obsession, he understood wanting something so bad, you went after it heart and soul.

Just because what he wanted out of life—retribution—wasn't concrete, it was still every bit as real as a brass bed. And coincidentally enough, what they both wanted was because of someone else. For Blaine, this bed was a gift for her sister. And for Donovan, retribution was for his mother.

But in an odd way, it was really for themselves. He'd have to be blind to not see that Blaine wanted that bed desperately for herself. And he knew damn well the retribution he desperately sought would also free his soul.

"Now you're worrying *me*," Blaine said softly, leaning back to look up into his face.

"Why?"

"*You've* stopped talking."

He smiled and let his gaze travel over her.

Her auburn hair flashed a deep fire where the light struck it. Her skin had the look of someone who spent time outdoors, but it wasn't just brown. It had a golden sheen. Shiny, alive. This wasn't one of those women who passively lay in the sun, slathering herself in some oily goop while "soaking" up some rays. No, Blaine was dynamic, vital. The type of woman who lived and breathed life, exerted herself with the elements.

"That bed," he finally said. "Why didn't you buy it for yourself?"

She rolled back her shoulders. "Because, as I told you, it's my sister's wedding gift."

He liked the sound of her voice, even when she was on her high horse. It had a throaty quality that reminded him of Courtney Cox, that TV actress his mom liked.

"But you love that bed. I see it in your face when you talk about it, hear it in your voice. Maybe you convinced *yourself* you bought it for your sister, but I think it should be a gift to you...for no other reason than you deserve something exquisite, beautiful." He lowered his voice. "Like you..."

He looked at the subtle tension in Blaine's expression. The way her green eyes darkened with a guardedness that watched him just as carefully as he was watching her. Then she turned her head, but not before he saw the glint of a tear in her eye.

"Hey," she said, a bit too casually, "why'd you check into this room if you knew the bed wasn't here?"

Raising her arm, she pressed the edge of a sleeve to her eye.

"Had no choice. They wouldn't let me just check the room, I had to check *into* it, too. So I paid eighty-five bucks plus tax to discover this room doesn't contain your bed."

He leaned over and gently touched another tear that spilled down her cheek. He then turned her face toward the feeble light from the window and cupped her cheek with his roughened hand. His thumb lazily grazed the side of her face as he stared into her eyes for a long moment.

"Ah, Blaine, sweet Blaine," he murmured.

If he teased her, or even yelled at her, she could keep the emotion in check. But, no, Donovan had to go all tender and caring on her. She tried to surreptitiously dab the edge of her T-shirt against her cheek to stop another tear.

"You're rubbing more dirt on your face by using your shirt," he said. "I'll get a tissue."

Wonderful, she thought as he exited to the bathroom. *At this affectionate, sensitive moment, I've been sitting here looking like a coalminer.*

He returned and crouched in front of her. Gently, he wiped a tissue along the glistening path of a fresh tear.

"I can take care of myself," she said feebly.

"You're so damn bullheaded," he whispered, pulling another tissue out of his pocket. He dabbed her cheeks, the corners of both eyes, then stayed close, inches from her face, staring into her eyes. "There's more dirt smudges on your face, but if you'd rather take care of them yourself..."

"No," she said a bit too quickly. "Uh, it just seems easier if you take care of me. I mean, my tears. After all, I don't have a mirror." Just at that moment, she glanced up and saw a mirror positioned on the ceiling over the bed. Her mouth dropped open.

He followed her gaze. "Well, you could lie on the bed and stare up at that mirror..."

She quickly looked back into Donovan's eyes. "I, uh, probably couldn't see the smudges from that far away."

He made a mock serious expression. "Good point. Plus the light in here isn't very good."

"Right," she said, suddenly finding it hard to catch a breath. "It's all hazy and red..." What would he look like naked in this light? Her heart suddenly picked up its pace, thumping double time.

He placed his hands on either side of her. The heat of his body radiated against her, triggering memories of last night's passion. She sucked in a deep breath, the motion lifting the thin material of her T-shirt, as she remembered how skilled his hands had been.

She licked her suddenly dry lips. "You're flirting with me," she whispered. "Right?"

He flashed her a funny look. "Don't you think men find you attractive?"

"Sure," she croaked. She cleared her throat. "But in case you haven't noticed, I'm more the tomboy type."

"Oh, really? I thought you were the fascinating type with more than her share of strength and spark."

A wave of heat spread through Donovan's body. At this moment, he wanted nothing more than to take that strength and spark and feel its breath, taste it, fondle it, bend it beneath him.

"My strength and spark?" she repeated breathlessly, the question imbued with such sweet yearning, that he suddenly realized she'd opened the door to her soul, just a little. Offered him a cautious entrance into the secret world of Blaine Saunders.

He studied her face for a long moment. What a shame no man had ever made a fuss over her, pampered her. "Have you always taken care of Sonja?"

Blaine looked surprised, then nodded. "Well, since after Mom died."

He thought about that bed, and how obviously Blaine loved it. He wondered what else she'd loved in life, but given to her sister instead. Reminded him of his mother and how she repressed her needs, her very essence, for the sake of her family.

"Maybe it's time to put Blaine first," he said carefully, weighing his words. Because he had a theory that people who never put themselves first were the ones who most deeply buried their truest selves. And if life was a gift, what a shame to bury such a treasure.

That heart-shaped chin jutted forward. "I put myself first," she said defensively.

"Oh yeah?"

"Yeah."

"Like when?"

He waited.

Silence.

"Open up for me, Blaine," he whispered. "Tell me who you are."

At first she looked startled. She blinked. "I'm..." Her voice was wispy, so unlike the bold, sassy tone he'd grown accustomed to. "I'm my sister's mother and her best friend, my father's caretaker and staunchest supporter, my family's glue. I'm my business's leader, my employees' confessor, motivator, parent, mentor..."

"So I was right."

"About what?"

"You never put yourself first. Everything is for your sister, your father, your business...but never for Blaine."

It was as though he was watching Blaine's façade crumble before his eyes. He'd dug too far. Penetrated some secret place she didn't share with others. Or maybe he'd hit on a truth she'd never admitted to herself.

"I don't want to talk anymore," she said in a choked voice.

Thunder erupted, a long angry rumble that tore apart the heavens. The rain splashed angrily against the window.

"I'm sorry." Donovan stood, tossed the tissues into a nearby basket and headed for the window. "That was a long hike you took getting here," he said, purposefully changing the subject. "You're gonna feel it tomorrow. A hot tub would help those cranky muscles." He nodded toward the back of the room.

"That pedestal is a hot tub?"

He frowned. "What?"

She smiled sheepishly. "I thought that thing in the back was a pedestal."

Blaine was standing. His gaze dipped, observing how her denim pants hugged her thighs, curving snugly in places he recalled from last night's dreamlike encounter. The sight, and the memories, slicked his palms with moisture. Damn, he wanted her again.

But just as he'd sworn to her this morning, he hadn't intended to take advantage of her. And he still meant it.

"By the way," he said casually, turning his back to her again, "I didn't mention the hot tub as a prelude to more."

"Oh," she said.

Was that disappointment in her voice?

"No," she continued, "I didn't think you meant that."

"I'll just move this ridiculously small couch around," he gestured toward the red-upholstered love seat, "and sit with my back to you. You're free to doff your clothes and jump into the tub undisturbed and to-tally safe. Only if you want to, of course."

"I'll give it a think."

There was such a long pause, he glanced over at her. Blaine stood in the center of the room, staring at the ceiling fan as though the answer was whirling within those blades. Yes, no, yes, no. She was funny. Wild and untamed one moment. All business the next.

And then, like a little girl counting petals on a flower. Only these were blades on a fan.

"Okay," she announced as though speaking to a roomful of people and not just Donovan.

Okay? He turned just in time to see her tug the bottom of her T-shirt out of her pants.

"I'm taking a hot tub because I'm putting myself first!"

6

BLAINE BEGAN PEELING OFF her T-shirt.

"Stop!" said Donovan, half choking on the word.

Gripping her shirt, which she'd raised to just beneath her breasts that were unconstrained by a bra, Blaine peered questioningly at Donovan. "Stop what?"

"Stop...taking off your clothes until I've, uh..." He made a vague gesture toward the couch, his gaze lowering to her exposed stomach. His brown eyes glistened like polished bronze. The room had air-conditioning, or she'd been aware of it at first, anyway.

But now the air seemed charged, hot, like the building storm outside.

And when he raised his eyes, she saw a hungry look in them. Like a man who'd been without food and water for days and days.

Thunder rumbled in the distance, its sound reverberating across the sky.

"Storm's getting closer," Donovan murmured, not bothering to look over his shoulder, his gaze riveted to her.

"It's almost here," she agreed, her breath like scattered wind.

Emotion thickened the air. Above her, the whir-whir-whir of the overhead fan mimicked the frantic beating of her heart. With Donovan's body bulk, disheveled hair and that unholy glint in his eye, he looked downright fierce, far more dangerous than any approaching storm.

And yet neither of them moved. They stood stockstill, staring at each other. And for a heart-stopping minute, she swore he was going to charge across the room, drag her into his arms and make mad, passionate, knock-over-furniture love to her.

She braced herself, waiting for the onslaught.

Nothing happened.

Not even a flick of his baby finger.

Was Donovan being a gentleman?

She released her grip on the T-shirt, dropping her hands to her sides.

For a moment Blaine wasn't sure whether to be impressed or thoroughly pissed. Okay, okay, the deal was she was putting herself first by hopping into the tub, but she'd have to be blindfolded not to see the steamy thoughts glistening in Donovan's eyes. Which only ignited her hot needs. Add their being in an X-rated motel, in a room that had "lovefest" written all over it, and it was a little rough on the ego to be told to *stop*.

Sheesh, she hadn't even exposed anything *good* yet.

Old memories, where guys at school teased Blaine for looking better in sweats than a dress, or throwing a ball better than a line, stabbed at her pride.

The way Donovan's rejection—well, it *felt* like a rejection—also stabbed at her pride. She probably should've just taken his suggestion—to hop into the tub—and not gotten caught up in hot looks and sizzling innuendoes.

Probably. But that wasn't Blaine's style to second-guess. She had to know for sure.

"Okay, here's the deal." She fisted her hands on her hips, acting tougher than she felt. "If...if I played this situation wrong, just tell it to me straight. Because I'm not one of those girly types who knows how to read between the lines." Her words gathered speed like a car racing downhill without brakes, but she couldn't stop herself. "Hell, I can't even take a hint. I suppose if Mom had lived longer, I'd have learned some of those feminine-protocol things, but she didn't and I didn't. So what you're left with is *me*, not Miss Manners, just plain ol' say-it-like-it-is Blaine Saunders."

There was such a long pause, she wondered if there was some kind of time warp and her words had yet to reach him across the room.

One dark eyebrow shot up. "You finished?" he asked.

"Yes."

Donovan folded his arms across his chest and cocked his head. "What in the hell are you talking about?"

If he'd looked angry, she'd have sputtered something else defensive, but even in the muted red light of the room, she could see that his eyes had turned a soft brown. Like the drawn-out days of summer before autumn. The time when the world turns benevolent, ready to change.

Donovan, benevolent?

It imbued him with an appeal she hadn't noticed before. For all his outward wrath and fury, the truth was, he was a sensitive guy.

"Uh…" she began, feeling a tad dumb for giving that little "here's the deal" speech. "I, uh, felt…" Don't say it. Don't say it. "Rejected." *I said it.*

He looked so confused, she instantly regretted being ol' say-it-like-it-is Blaine. Maybe, after her business got on its feet again and she had some cash to spare, she should sign up for one of those etiquette classes like her sister Sonja did years ago. Learn to speak politely, wear gloves, buy frilly dresses.

Nah. She just needed to stop blurting out things. Screw the polite-glovey-dressy part.

"Rejected?" Donovan drew his brows together. "Because I told you to not take off your shirt?"

She nodded. "Silly, huh?" she croaked. *Please say it's silly.*

As though he read her mind, his mouth curved into a smile. A sweetly amused smile. The kind that made a girl's heart melt into a puddle at her feet.

"Sweet, sweet Blaine," he said in a deep, throaty voice. He leaned one hip against the back of the love seat as he stared intently at her. "Only a crazy man would reject you."

And then Donovan smiled, *really* smiled, which involved his entire mouth. So strong, so beautiful, it was like a jolt of lightning.

It brought back that flash of feeling she'd had this morning—the morning after their sinfully hot, dreamy encounter. When she'd been sitting in his kitchen, indulging in a moment of crazy love-at-first-sight.

The kind of feeling she'd never believed in.

Well, never believed in before Donovan.

"You are a very beautiful woman, Blaine." His gaze boldly raked over her. "I still remember..." He made a barely audible sound of pleasure. "I'll *always* remember...no, savor...my memories of a dazzling, passionate woman."

Dazzling? Passionate? If someone had stunned her with a cattle prod, she couldn't have been as dumbstruck speechless. These compliments were like a mind-altering elixir. And better yet, it was how he *said* it. Tinged with wonder, as though she were the first woman he'd ever uttered them to in his entire life.

No, the first woman with whom he'd shared such an experience.

Nahhhhh. A hunky stud muffin like Donovan surely had had his share of bedmates. All kinds of dazzling, passionate ones. Except...maybe...just maybe he was talking this way because he had experienced that irrational, but deliciously real, blast of love at first sight, too?

Blaine closed her eyes, basking in the moment, his words, wanting to remember them forever...to relish how it felt to be the object of a man's adoration. To be beautiful for herself, not for other feminine ideals. Remember, remember...

"Thank you," she finally whispered, opening her eyes.

Looking at his smoldering gaze, a tension coiled

tightly inside her. She ached to feel him, taste him again...

Through the window behind Donovan, she saw dark storm clouds hovering over Pikes Peak, flashes of lightning tearing the sky with jagged bolts of yellow and blue.

Just like the weather, maybe she should put on more of a show, too. Show him what she wanted. Not fear rejection.

She popped the first button on her jeans.

He swallowed so hard, she swore she saw his Adam's apple work up and down. "I told you I wouldn't take advantage of you," he said in a strangled voice. He was staring at her breasts again, working one of his hands as though virtually fondling her.

She paused. "And you haven't." So that's why he'd held back. Just as he'd said this morning, he never took advantage of a woman. Through his inaction, she was understanding Donovan more and more. Now she felt the confidence to do what she wanted. To blast that stupid "taking advantage" notion right out of his head.

She raised her gaze from his twitching hand back to his eyes. Maintaining a bold eye contact with him, she played slowly with the next button. Twisting it a little, fingering it as though it just might go through the slit.

Was that a red flush creeping up his neck?

Oh, yes. She *loved* how the ruddy stain colored his neck and filled his cheeks. Those rugged, whiskered cheeks. She'd never seen a man go hot over one little manipulated button.

How would he react if she played with other little manipulations, like words?

"Something's always bothered me on those strip joint signs," she said innocently, "where they advertise 'totally nude' women. What's the 'totally' part? Are they nude or aren't they?"

She popped open the button.

Donovan opened his mouth, but all that came out was a slow, hissing sound as though all the air had seeped out of his body. His mouth tried to assume its familiar sullen slant, but failed. Instead, his lips formed a sort of lopsided grin. The kind she'd seen Harrison Ford give a hundred times in every movie he'd ever made.

Except it looked a hell of a lot better on Donovan.

He shifted his weight from one foot to the other, as though he would burst outta those jeans any moment.

She was getting to him, big time. Blaine loved the thrill of this new experience, teasing a man to the point where he was blushing and near-bursting.

"It's an interesting topic, don't you think?" she said coyly, playing with the next button on her jeans. "Nude versus totally nude."

"Damn it, Blaine," he said through gritted teeth. "I'm moving the damn couch because if I don't, I'm stuck standing here, watching you...and it makes me crazy watching you undress, getting..."

Makes him crazy? "Getting *almost* undressed," she corrected teasingly. "Not *totally*."

"And you wondered what the difference was between nude and totally nude," he growled.

"Still don't know. Think somebody could write a dissertation on the subject?"

"I'm a..." His eyes dropped to her fingers playing with the button. "...a computer scientist, not a linguist."

She stopped toying with the button. "You have a *doctorate?*"

He nodded.

Her whole hotsie-totsie act went on hold as she stared at him in amazement. She dropped her gaze to his scuffed boots, up his well-worn jeans with the rip across one knee, back to that rugged face. Not that she didn't think he was smart, it was just rare to find a rough and rugged cowboy-looking type who also had a *doctorate*. It was like discovering Tom Cruise was also a nuclear physicist.

"What're you doing living like a pauper?" she blurted. "You have a Ph.D. in computer science, for God's sake. It's people like you who can rake in the big bucks—" She stopped herself before blundering on that he could surely afford a heck of a lot more than a faded yellow-and-brown plaid recliner and a bookshelf made of bricks and planks.

After a long moment, Donovan finally said, "Pauper? Maybe shunning money is the beginning of true wealth."

Oooh, a deep thinker. Definitely the doctorate type. "But..."

"But what?"

She blew out a puff of air. "It's just that..." Oh, to hell with it. She was too damn curious not to ask. "You're such a loner. One look at your place and it's obvious you eat alone, listen to music alone, read alone. Why? What's that old saying? No man's an island?'' She clamped shut her mouth, but too late. She'd already blurted everything on her mind and then some.

''Excuse me if I don't respond quickly. I'm trying to assimilate your barrage of words.''

Blaine tried to smile, but felt a little sick inside. *I've gone from ''beautiful'' to ''barrage.''*

''I live alone, yes,'' he began, choosing his words carefully, ''because...I'm a cautious man. I prefer to protect myself and what's mine.''

But Blaine sensed he was leaving the most critical part out—that to open his world meant risking something...

Like his spirit?

Whatever had happened to hurt him, he held it close the way a card player holds a killer hand. The secret in Donovan's cards could make or break him.

Her gaze traveled over the man who was part intellectual, part cowboy, wondering if she'd ripped apart the mood with her questions. Well, it was in his court now. She lost the heart to play games anymore.

He was just so damn different than anybody she'd ever met. So *introspective.* She'd once heard someone say that spoken words, although invisible, were actually objects, as real as a piece of furniture, and where they were spoken, they stayed forever.

She had the sense that words had that kind of impact with Donovan, too. Whatever was said to him, or had been said to him, pierced his world with the impact of a bullet. He kept words close, she'd guess, and reviewed them the way he read his books or listened to his music.

Slowly. Methodically.

She made a mental note to herself to try really, really hard to not blurt out whatever was on her mind with Donovan from here on out. This was bucking a lifetime habit, but she'd try.

When she looked into his face again, he looked so expectant...as though he were ready to say something.

"Hungry?" he finally asked.

She smiled, relieved the topic had veered onto a safer course. "Famished."

Donovan was ravenous, too. More sexually hungry than physically, but he needed to put on some brakes. Things had heated up again in this room, then Blaine had blindsided him with some questions that drilled beyond lust and tore right into his core.

He needed to slow things down, breathe, figure out what the hell the two of them were getting themselves into.

Plus, last night had been wild, out of control. Not that he couldn't handle that, but if they went that route again, he'd like to remember more than hazy, fragmented pieces of a scorching dream. Which wasn't a bad thing, but he hadn't been with a woman, *really* been with a woman, in over a year...he wanted to hold on to the memories, which meant he had to make them first.

Yeah, time to take it slow.

"When'd you last eat?" he asked.

"Oh..." There was a long pause. "Picked up a chicken mc-something on my way over to your place last night."

"That's *all* you've had in the last twenty-four hours?"

"No, there was more. Topped it off with superlarge fries, enough ketchup to qualify as a vegetable, a vanilla shake with those little chocolate sprinkle things all mixed in. And for dessert, a box of red vines."

"Red vines?"

"You know, those nonfat raspberry-flavored strips of chewy stuff."

He paused. It didn't sound like a meal, it sounded like a mess. "You ate some nonfat 'red vines' after a fat-glutted, fast-food meal?"

"I have a high metabolism."

He looked her up and down. "That I believe," he murmured, thinking about all the ways that hot little body could burn up calories.

"Not that I couldn't be persuaded to indulge in a gooey chocolate dessert, but I have a thing for red vines. I like how sweet, juicy and chewy they are."

Sugary, fire-hot sensations rolled over him. If she repeated the words "sweet, juicy and chewy" one more time, he'd have a hell of a time taking this slow.

"Too bad there isn't a McDonald's next door."

In the past, the women he'd dated ate so many salads, he felt as though they were grazing, not eating. God forbid an ounce of fat might pass their lips. But Blaine? He should've known she'd be different.

Smiling, he gave his head a shake. He'd never been

with a fast-food junkie before. Made him wonder what other indulgences she had. "You craving fast food again?"

"Even if there was a place nearby, I wouldn't let you drive through a downpour just to pick up fries and a shake."

But for her, he probably would. He'd drive through a downpour, a storm. He'd probably go through hell it-self just for one of her pixieish, life-affirming smiles.

Go through hell? He blinked. *Whoa, buddy, rein it in.* It was one thing to view Blaine as special, but he needed to mentally step back, assess the big picture.

"Something wrong?" Blaine asked.

"My life isn't just a full plate, it's piled high and spilling over the sides."

She flashed him a confused look. "How'd we go from being hungry to your life on plates?"

He started to answer, but stopped himself. How could he explain the last year? How over a year ago, af-ter earning his doctorate, he'd been on the verge of landing a "big bucks" job, but instead returned home to help his mom. How he'd spent the last year earning money to satisfy creditors who were salivating like wolves to sink their teeth into what remained of the family ranch.

How he'd spent these last, long months so rock-bot-tom lonely he'd sometimes ached for just a simple con-versation. But no matter how bad it got, he'd never pursued a woman, or even rung up an old friend, be-cause his energy was laser-focused on salvaging the ranch.

Yet, in the last day, all the upheaval and difficulties of the past year had faded into the background. For the first time since he'd returned to Colorado, he felt the ghost of the man he used to be—alive, happy, on the verge of taking over the world—lurking in the shadows, waiting for Donovan to welcome him back.

But he doubted he could be anything else until he'd straightened out the mess his father had left after his death.

And Donovan was musing about forging through hell for a lady's smile?

That was too damn close to actually forging a life with a lady, and he had zero room in his life for another commitment.

That's why he had his boundaries.

His heart contracted. Maybe that's what he should do now—define more boundaries, build more walls, before Blaine got too invested in whatever was going on between them. The nicest thing he could do for Blaine at this very moment would be to walk out the door.

He scraped a hand across his jaw, not wanting to look at her, not wanting to feel the rushes of heat and need that she aroused in him.

It was getting tough standing in this room, talking to Blaine and her red-tinged body, thoughts swirling in his head like that overheated water in the tub.

"I have some leftovers in my car," he said. "Beef jerky, maybe an apple or two." He paused. "Before I go, I'll take the cover off the hot tub, check the water. Make sure it's ready for you...when you're ready."

Blaine chewed on her bottom lip, confused by Donovan's switch of tone. He suddenly seemed all business. Getting food, checking the tub. It was probably because she'd asked about his loner lifestyle. She felt somewhat bad for asking things, but not bad enough to take them back. She knew Donovan intimately, sexually, but damn it all...she wanted to know more than just the physical.

She wanted to know his heart, too.

But to get there, she was having to wind her way through the labyrinth of his emotions and personality twists.

As though she were easy to figure out.

She gave her head a shake. What a combo they were. He, cautious. She, speedy. He despised rules, she worshipped them. He built barriers as though fortresses were going out of style. Her life was like a revolving door, with all kinds of people going in and out.

But their differences also made for a great chemistry. In fact, if opposites attract, she sensed their differences were downright combustible.

Donovan was bustling around the hot tub. "Temperature feels about right," he said.

"Thanks."

He walked stiffly past her, his eyes zeroed in on the front door. "I'll go to my truck now. Be back in a few."

He brushed by close enough that she could smell his scent. Could almost sense his pulsing heartbeat, the heat of his skin. Her heart exploded into a breathless tempo as she watched the confident swagger of his walk.

Blaine lifted her hand, her fingers eagerly spread, but he escaped her reach. Her hand hung in midair for a moment, then dropped. And for a cold moment she felt a miserable sense of loss.

He reached the door, placed his hand on the knob then glanced over his shoulder.

His eyes were filled with such a tormented wistfulness, her heart ached.

And in a flash, she knew that his ambivalence wasn't a matter of whether he desired her. Or didn't want to take advantage of her.

He's acting this way because his attraction to me threatens his world.

He opened the door, his bulk silhouetted against a backdrop of turbulent gray sky. Then he stepped outside, the door clicking solidly shut behind him.

She contemplated Donovan for a long moment, debating what to do.

"If tonight's temporary," she finally whispered to herself, "so be it." She'd take that challenge because at a deep, gut level, she sensed that opening Donovan's tightly guarded heart held a reward she'd treasure for the rest of her life.

HE DASHED OUTSIDE, grateful for the onslaught of wet, cold rain. He needed out of that room, fast, and he didn't care that rain sluiced over him, drenching him. He just stood for a moment outside, letting the elements pound some sense into his fevered state.

The air swirled violently. In the distance, he heard

the shriek of a bird, the impending storm surprising it out of its sanctuary.

God knows Donovan had lived through his share of summer storms around Manitou. He couldn't even count the number of times he'd battled high winds, torrential rains, lightning. But this time, the storm was more than just nature's fury unleashing.

It was as though the outside world mirrored his interior one. And for a blazing moment, he gave in to those feelings—fury, anxiety and wild, potent desire—that knotted his insides. This whole damn bed-and-Blaine experience was opening him up to emotions, needs he hadn't experienced in years. Things he'd held at bay for so long were tearing into him like the wind and rain. Breaking down his walls, destroying his defenses.

Damn her.

He hunched his shoulders and jogged to his pickup, not wanting to feel more. He jumped inside, grateful to get out of the rain. He pulled the car keys out of his jeans pocket and stuck them in the ignition.

I should leave...

He fiddled with the key. One sharp twist, the engine would turn, he'd be outta here...before he left, he'd make a call at the front desk, request a taxi pick her up so she'd get home safely.

And he'd drop back into the room, quicklike, tell her he was sorry, but a ride was on its way. Avoid the look of surprise and hurt that would inevitably shadow her sweet face.

Avoid the ache that would inevitably stab at his heart.

The rain pounded against the truck, the world outside a gray, wet haze. Thunder growled, taunting him.

He reared back and banged his hand against the steering wheel.

Damn boundaries.

Were they there to protect his life or to prevent him from feeling anything again?

He looked at the rain sheeting down his driver's window, flowing effortlessly to its destination. He constantly reminded himself to go with the flow. Well, where did he want to go?

7

THE DOOR REOPENED WITH A whoosh, the scent of rain and earth rushing in with the man.

"The hunter returns!" Donovan announced, stepping inside. "A bag of beef jerky, Twinkies, and to wash it down..." He waved a pint in the air, the clear liquid sparkling red from the room light. "Tequila!"

"It's a feast!" Blaine concurred, happy to see the dark, troubled look in his eyes was gone.

As was his shirt.

"What happened to the doughnut shirt?" she asked, checking out the plain white T-shirt he now wore. Make that plain white with a tear at the shoulder. Ripped jeans. Ripped T-shirts. His clothes were beginning to remind her of his seen-better-days furniture.

He set the food and tequila on the glass coffee table in front of the love seat. "Got soaked on the way to the truck so while grabbing food, I changed shirts."

"You keep clothes in your truck?"

"Since I'm constantly going to the ranch to help out, I keep spare clothes and snacks in the pickup."

"To the ranch," she repeated. Images of him working outside, shirtless, explained his tan, chiseled chest and muscled arms.

She inhaled deeply, smelling the wet tannin of his

boots. And his familiar masculine scent. How would he taste if she ran her tongue over his rain-drenched skin?

She could sense how they were struggling to remain themselves, to "act" normal—whatever that meant—but they were on the edge of something new...and she was ready to let go, be someone different, discover whatever secrets Donovan was ready to reveal...or show her.

"So that's where the computer scientist gets his buff," she said.

"Buff?" He arched one eyebrow, then shot her a cocky half smile that made her insides do funny things. "Yes, I suppose I get 'buffed' from fixing fences, doing house repairs, riding horses..." Sitting down on the red velvet love seat, he winced slightly and rubbed the spot on his leg.

It was a slight movement, almost absentminded, but from what Blaine could tell, he was definitely touching some kind of physical wound. She thought back, trying to remember if she'd noticed anything on his leg this morning that indicated an injury. But there had been no gashes, cuts...no bandages covering anything, either.

"Is your leg hurting?"

"Old break," he answered, quickly withdrawing his hand from the spot.

His tone of voice had "Do Not Enter" all over it.

Maybe she should be cautious herself...adopt a "Do Not Go There" philosophy. Because maybe the last thing she needed was to stack yet another temporary incident onto her life. Because being with Donovan, getting more involved, could mean diving into something hot that could flame and disappear like rising steam.

Okay, okay, maybe she was jumping to conclusions here. After all, who'd said they were on the road to *sharing* their lives?

But when she flashed back on the past twenty-four hours with this man, something in her gut said this was way more than a one-night fling. Maybe it wasn't so bizarre those feelings she'd had this morning. Those hit by lightning, love-at-first-sight feelings.

His brows furrowed, as though he were trying to read her thoughts. Poor guy was probably as confused as she was.

Finally Donovan said, "Maybe it would be wise for us to forget about..."

"Right," she said, trying to sound matter-of-fact. "Maybe it's better if we just..." She made a dismissive motion with her hand.

He blew out a gust of air. Straightening, he shot her a look. "Know what I *really* think?" he suddenly said, his eyes glistening. "We're thinking too damn much. A common fault of mine, I'll admit. We're here, dinner's on the table, let's enjoy ourselves and not analyze everything to death."

He patted a spot on the couch next to him.

Let's enjoy ourselves. The way he patted that red-velvet seat, indicating she should sit there right next to his hard, jean-straining thigh, was doing wicked things to her libido. It didn't help that the room's red light

played glorious tricks with his rich brown locks, exposing glints of gold, like hidden secrets.

"So," she said, taking the few steps toward him,
"you're a combo cowboy, computer scientist, construc-
tion worker?" Add a policeman and she'd personally
enlarge that rip in his T-shirt with her bare teeth.

She sat on the love seat with a very unladylike
whoomp. Damn, the postage-size seat was so small, it
was a miracle she'd landed on it at all. Plus the cushion
was lumpy, causing her body to tilt so that her left side
pressed firmly against him. She tried to regain some
semblance of balance, well sort of tried. After some
twisting and turning, she ended up even more angled
toward him, her elbow wrenched somewhere near his
ribs, her chin nearly resting on that ripped-shirt shoulder.

He chuckled. "You okay?"

Hell no. "Yes."

"I suppose I'm all three."

"All three what?" she said, realizing her lips could
almost touch his ear. When she spoke, a tuft of his rich
molasses brown hair, the tuft that curled provocatively
down his rich brown neck, wavered slightly.

"All three jobs."

"Oh yeah. Jobs." If she stuck out her tongue just a little, she could even lick his earlobe. "Which job..." Hell,
better yet, if she turned her head just a tad, she could
suckle that lobe. "...do you get paid for?" Like she
cared. Like she even knew what she was talking about
anymore. Like the word "blurt" even existed in her vo-
cabulary.

"Computer scientist. The others are what I do to help out my mom on the ranch, or what's left of it."

She heard a warning in his voice. *Do Not Enter*, Blaine reminded herself. *Don't ask more about the ranch.*

She pulled back and looked up into his eyes, which had darkened to an unfathomable, murky brown. Yeah, he'd definitely put up the Do Not Enter sign. Time to focus on something else. Like food.

But suddenly, the last thing she wanted was to eat. Maybe before she'd been famished, but how could a girl eat when her senses were on overload with the sounds of a man's honey-roughened voice and the scents of his clean, manly self?

She needed something to calm her nerves, fast.

She snatched the opened bottle of tequila off the table in front of them. "Cheers!" She downed a sip. Blaine smiled as she lowered the bottle, enjoying how the liquid felt like gentle fire as it trickled lazily down her throat.

"Stop!"

She lowered the bottle.

"Maybe you shouldn't mix allergy medications with alcohol."

And maybe you shouldn't reek of primal masculinity. She stared at him over the edge of the bottle, vaguely aware her tongue was playing with its lip. "It was a six-hour pill, which has already worn off," she answered, barely recognizing her own voice which had dipped into some primitive, needy range. She cleared her throat. "Besides, my allergies aren't bothering me thanks to the rain."

She took another sip. A long one.

He looked at the bottle, then back into her eyes. "You probably should have partaken of some food first. You like Twinkies?"

"Sweets to the sinful," she muttered, licking a drop of tequila off her bottom lip.

"Huh?"

"Uh, I'd better not start off with dessert. All that sugar, I'll be bouncing off the walls."

"Jerky, then?"

She bit her lip to stop herself from blurting something she'd regret.

"Gotta warn you, it's spicy," he said. "Fire-hot jalapeño flavored."

"Get me a fire extinguisher." She took another sip of tequila, not taking her eyes off his lips. She loved how they moved when he talked, like he was taking little bites off words. Her pulse raced remembering the little nibbles he'd taken of her last night....

"Care for some?" He held up the bag of jerky.

She glanced at the bag and the big, green pepper emblazoned on its front. "Maybe I'll start with Twinkies, after all. What's a little wall bouncing? No, wait, knowing you, the Twinkies are probably habañero-filled and I'll never be the same."

He eased the bottle from her fingers and took a chug. After swallowing, he said, "Well, I promise it's not habañero. And I have the feeling that after knowing you, it's *me* who'll never be the same."

Donovan hadn't meant to say that. He never spoke without knowing exactly what he wanted to express...and yet, he'd just done exactly that. Revealed more than he intended. No, this had nothing to do with intention. He'd revealed something he hadn't been aware of, consciously anyway.

But now that he'd said it, he knew it to be true. He'd never be the same. Somehow this little package of dynamo had blasted through his barriers. Not just his apartment and his bed, but his psyche, too.

No, she hadn't blasted through.

He'd let her in. Willingly.

A moment of panic swept over him. He, who liked having his guard up, had opened himself to a woman he barely knew?

No, not barely. Blaine was more than that. Much more. He wasn't a man drawn to mysticism, but from the moment they touched, it was as though they'd been soldered by the fates.

Lightning crackled and sizzled outside.

But daring to be vulnerable also meant he was forced to experience a torrent of feelings, everything from excitement to apprehension. Emotions as fierce and harsh as the storm outside.

He took another sip, not wanting to think about his life anymore. Lowering the bottle, he said, "So tell me why you cashed in your cruise ticket to Alaska for that bed."

It took Blaine by surprise for a moment, then she recalled how this morning she'd mentioned refunding her cruise ticket to buy her sister's wedding gift.

So Blaine summarized the story of her Alaskan dream cruise—how it was something she'd wanted to do ever since writing a report on the northern lights back in grade school, and how she'd gleefully cashed in this year's income tax refund to buy a cruise ticket. Then, after David's surprise engagement announcement, how she cashed in the ticket for the brass bed.

Donovan chuckled. "No wonder you're crazy for that bed. Maybe that cruise was a dream, but I'd wager that bed is an even bigger dream for you."

At first she felt defensive and wanted to say something snappy about how it was her sister's wedding gift, not Blaine's dream, but the truth was, Donovan had hit the proverbial nail on the head.

"Yes," she confessed, "that bed represents a bigger dream to me." But she refused to say that it represented everything she felt she wasn't. Exotic, sensual, sexually adventurous. Just because he'd hit the nail on the head didn't mean she had to help him pound it all the way in.

"You're lucky," he continued, handing her back the bottle. "You have a dream."

"And you don't? Doesn't everybody have a dream?"

"No. Not me, anyway." He paused. "Well, maybe. A long time ago. But that's gone. What's done is done."

She heard it in his voice. Resignation. "What did you give up?"

"Tangentially?" He stared off into the distance. "A six-figure income, plus perks," he said matter of factly. "A loft in Tribeca, a Benz or two, and later on, a trophy wife."

"Not that you've given it much thought..."

"Well, when you're at Princeton, top of your class in

a high-demand field, with major corporations throwing money at you as enticements to work for them, it's easy to imagine having the best life has to offer."

"A trophy wife? That's the best?"

He shrugged. "I was caught up in the external trappings of success. Mind you, I graduated with the doctorate only two years ago...then spent a year taking the odd consulting gig, seeing which corporation would offer the best employment bid, but I never had the opportunity to see if the loft, Benz, and trophy-wife wanna-bes were all they were trumped up to be."

"Why not?"

His expression tightened. "My world turned upside down. Then I gave up."

"You...don't seem like a man who's given up."

"That's not what I meant." His face clouded over. "I gave up on people. Gave up on believing in them."

"Somebody must have pounded you pretty good for you to give that up."

"Pounded?" He made a derisive sound. "I had my share of fistfights in my day, but nobody pounded that little truth into me." He started to take another sip of tequila, but stopped. "Sometimes words have more force than a fist."

She held her breath, almost disbelieving he had said what she'd been thinking earlier. How words could have a shattering impact on Donovan. But she held her tongue.

Because to say anything at this moment meant she risked his growing silent, retreating within himself the way he retreated within that cave he called home.

She observed how the red light glazed over him, casting him in a more dangerous light. If Blaine were to tell him how he appeared at this moment, he'd probably like it. Looking dangerous was undoubtedly another way of erecting a boundary, keeping people away.

Except her. For tonight, anyway.

His changing moods had thrown her off tonight, but in her gut, she knew he wanted her here. Needed her. Again, she sensed their connection, sensed his emotions. Determination. Anger. And in a deeper sense, despair at being locked in a world where he was so alone.

She hesitated a moment, watching his profile. More than ever, she wanted to be with him, release him from his troubles, make love to him.

Fiery, passionate love. The kind that burns away the world's petty worries.

"It's getting awfully hot in here," she whispered.

He looked around the room for a thermostat. "Want me to turn down the—" But when he glanced back at Blaine, he knew she wasn't talking about the temperature. "Well..." he said, measuring his words, reminding himself he'd wanted to take things slowly.

He glanced at Blaine's T-shirt, recalling she'd said it read NASCAR Roars when she'd had a chance to dress "properly." "What do you want?" he asked, knowing damn well any lady who loved fast cars undoubtedly loved other things fast, too. Take it slow, he counseled himself, wondering if he could.

Blaine shifted in her seat. Outside, the rush of rain and wind sounded like someone whispering "lovers."

Lovers.

"What do I want?" Emboldened by the tequila, and her fired-up libido, Blaine leaned close and whispered, "I want to devour you like a fast-food manwich."

While Donovan's jaw dropped, she abruptly stood.

Not a swift move.

She teetered a bit for balance, before finding her footing. She stepped over the table, vaguely thinking that most women would probably have walked *around* the furniture, then turned and faced Donovan, her breasts at his eye level. In one swift motion, she yanked the shirt over her head and tossed it aside.

"Oh, God, baby…" Donovan rasped, his brown eyes widening.

She sucked in a breath, which plumped up her mounds just that much more.

He made a tormented sound.

Blaine had often experienced the thrill of winning against men in sports, but never the exhilaration of winning over a man as her lover. She dropped back her head, sighing as a rush of cool air washed over her. Refreshing, soothing. Plus, those little ripples of air from the overhead fan were doing deliciously naughty things to her chest. Her nipples went all perky, the pink buds springing to life. Oh yeah, that overhead fan was working wonders on her hot, needy breasts. Cooling, stroking, teasing them…

She raised her head. A trickle of sweat coursed between her mounds. "You wouldn't happen to have another tissue, would you?"

"No," he answered in a choked voice. "Threw what I had in the trash."

"Too bad." She slowly trailed a finger down her chest, slipping it between her breasts, and with a flick of her finger, wiped the trail of moisture. "Thought you could dab me dry, the way you did my tears."

His lips parted, and he emitted a low, rumbling groan like a wounded animal. His eyes smoldered, his chest heaved. The red lights in the room gilded his profile, giving him a forbidden, lusty appearance.

"You are one drop-dead gorgeous lady," he finally murmured, the words rumbling from deep in his chest.

Honest to God, she could feel his heat across the space between them, right through her skin, down to her marrow. No guy, *ever*, had used those words to describe Blaine. *Drop-dead gorgeous*. Not even in a desperate fit of wanting to get into her panties had some guy even tried that line.

That lock of hair had fallen over his forehead again. Her gaze dropped to his seriously sexy mouth and the way his features hardened with undisguised need. And those eyes...the most expressive part of his face. Sometimes burning with fury, sometimes shining with amusement.

But right now, they scorched her with a relentless intensity.

Outside, thunder rumbled. Like an animal on the prowl, the sound snarled and roared across the skies, finally skulking off into the distance with a threatening growl.

She'd buttoned her pants back up when he'd left to get the food. Now she grabbed the top of her jeans and tugged, hard, the buttons making a pop-pop-pop sound as they flew open.

She kicked off her sneakers and shimmied out of her jeans. Then, with another brisk tug, she whisked off her undies—wishing they were prettier than the plain cotton ones she always wore—and tossed them aside.

With a sassy turn, she walked across the thick, plush rug to the back of the room. To the hot tub. Sitting on its cool edge, she twiddled her fingers in the water. "Mmm," she murmured, "nice 'n hot."

Had Donovan just groaned again or was that distant thunder?

She swung her legs around, submerging them in the steamy water. Wet, hot bubbles tickled her calves. "Oh, God," she moaned, leaning back and paddling her legs ever so slowly in the delicious warmth. "This...is... heaven."

She slipped her entire body into the water, submerging herself to her neck, groaning with the sheer pleasure of liquid heat stroking every single inch of her body. Water hissed and sputtered around her ears and she giggled before dunking her head underneath the swirling turmoil.

It was strangely quiet under the surface. She shook her head, reveling in the sensation of her body floating weightlessly. The glimmer of red lights twinkling on the water's surface.

Then she sat up, breaking the surface of the water, and settled her rump on some plastic underwater ledge. Taking a deep breath, she swiped the drops of water off her face.

Blinking, she peered across the room.

Donovan stood in front of the window, just where the drapes parted. His dark form outlined sharply against the glow in the window. Broad shoulders. Narrow hips. And even from across the room, she could discern the wild mane of hair that looked about as uncontrollable as the man.

Thunder rumbled across the skies, reminding her of Donovan's voice. Low, rough, deliciously dangerous...

She stared at him, feeling bold and aroused. Her heart beat furiously, its drumming mixing with the swirling, sloshing water. "It's too light in here."

Donovan cocked his head. "There's barely enough light to see," he said incredulously.

She held her breath, then released it in a slow, raggedy rush. "Close the drapes," she said, raising her voice. "Then take off your clothes and get into the tub. We'll eat dinner over here." She licked her lips, pleased how she'd spoken up for herself. Put her needs first.

There was a long moment of silence.

"Yes, ma'am," Donovan finally said. The drapes closed, submerging the room in a dark, red haze.

Donovan stood in front of the closed drapes, staring across the room at the shimmering, scarlet-tinged image of Blaine naked in the tub. If there was such a thing as a lust-dipped oasis, Blaine was it.

With the curtains drawn, the room was cloaked once

again in shadows, the only light being spots of red, like pinpoints of heat.

And they all seemed drawn to Blaine.

Transfixed, he stared at her rosy-hued body, and the dots of water—sparkling like red sequins—on her face and chest. Blaine's hair, wet and shiny, was pulled back from her face. That sweet, impish face that stared at him, so open, so ready.

She was like an oasis for a man who'd been traveling for miles, years, starved for the touch of a woman.

Blaine raised her hand, water trickling from it, and crooked her finger in a "come here" gesture.

His heart kicked hard against the wall of his chest. Blood roared in his ears. And in a heat-drenched moment, he imagined dragging her luscious body out of that water, throwing her on the bed, and having his way with her...again and again...burying himself into that luscious mound of wet, hot...

He fisted his hands. No, he wouldn't rush it. He'd do it right, not create another foggy set of memories like last night. Tonight he wanted to make the kind of memories that a man could retrieve when life threw a sucker punch and he needed to remember something sweet and fiery and comforting.

He grabbed the food and bottle and headed across the room to the nightstand, positioned a few feet from the hot tub, and stood in the arc of its red glow. After setting down his bounty on the stand, he pulled off his T-shirt and tossed it aside.

Blaine's gaze hungrily traveled over his torso. Damn, had she noticed before how much hair swirled on that muscled chest of his? It looked wild, rampant, defying to be tamed.

He unzippered his pants halfway, then pulled back the fly…just enough to display what appeared to be a pair of tight, see-through mesh underwear, the stretchy material clinging mercilessly to his gorged member.

Externally, a cowboy. Internally, a scientist. But if a man were judged by his underwear, he was a Chippendale tease.

She heard a sound. A low, throaty growl like an animal on the hunt. Aggressive and unabashedly sexual. Belatedly, she realized the sound came from *her*.

"Hold on, baby," Donovan said, his voice so lethally sexy she had to grip the side of the hot tub for support. "We'll get there, but we're taking our time."

He finished unzipping his pants, taking waaay too long in her opinion. He kicked off his boots and socks, then in one smooth motion, stepped out of his jeans.

Which left him standing there, dressed in nothing but those mesh-clingy briefs that looked like some kind of lethal gift wrapping on one hell of a scrumptious package.

Sitting low in the tub, Blaine felt as though she were kneeling before him. She looked up, amazed at how large he looked standing there. A man bigger than life, like one of those mythological gods she'd studied in school years ago.

The only sound was the swirling tub water, the drumbeat of rainfall, and if she listened very, very carefully, their deviant breaths, ragged and restless.

Without thinking, she sloshed some water on her naked breasts as though that would cool them down.

"What next?" he asked suggestively.

She braced her arms against the side of the tub, ready to lean forward and tear off that stretchy number with her bare teeth when Donovan spoke again.

"The jerky or the Twinkies?"

She paused, her body rigid, prepared to lunge. "That's what you meant by 'what's next'?" she croaked.

"Right. Dinner. What's our first course? The jerky or the Twinkies?"

"You're killing me," she whispered, sliding back into the water. But she was famished. For sex, for food. Anyway, as she'd learned in sports, it was always best to eat ahead of time to keep up one's strength.

Because tonight she planned to be very, very strong.

8

"JERKY?" ASKED DONOVAN.

"Tease," murmured Blaine, staring at him with a look that was downright primal.

Blaine, you animal, Donovan thought with a smile. If he didn't watch it, this little lady would consume *him* before the food.

He ripped the bag open with his teeth, then dipped inside and pulled out a strip of the dried meat. "Open your mouth."

He leaned over and slid the food between those plump little lips that glistened candy-apple red in the lamplight, then helped himself to a strip of jerky. Holding it between his teeth, he shucked his underwear and kicked it aside.

Then he watched Blaine check him out. The way she chewed on her jerky while observing his member with big, round eyes got him even harder. Hell, if he felt self-important about anything, it was about his mind, not his size. He'd gotten his fair share in the male anatomy department, but the way Blaine looked at him, her face filled with wonder and awe, right now he swore his prick could cast a shadow across the entire state of Colorado.

He'd already caught her checking him out this

morning, but it seemed the lady could never get enough...

And as though making her wait was the punishment of the century, she heaved a long-suffering sigh.

He smiled. Oh, yeah, Blaine was special all right. Without a word, she'd just made him feel like the biggest, baddest loverboy this side of the Rockies.

Grabbing the bag with the remaining jerky and the plastic-wrapped Twinkies in one hand, the bottle of tequila with the other, Donovan stepped into the water and eased down on an underwater seat. For a moment, that old break in his leg twinged and he paused, waiting for the pain to pass.

Then he set the food and bottle on the floor, next to the tub.

Underneath the water, their legs rubbed against each other. Liquid, silky sensations. He felt his groin tighten and imagined how good it was going to be.

She finished chewing, then coughed a little. "That jerky was spicy!" She blew out a breath, flapped her hand in front of her mouth as though that would cool off the heat she'd consumed then grabbed another strip. "No prob, though. I can handle it."

Just like Blaine to meet a challenge.

"I like hot things," he explained.

"Me, too." As she chewed, she gave him a wickedly devilish look. Electricity that could outdo any blast of lightning sizzled between them.

Finished eating, Blaine said, "Pass the tequila, please."

He purposefully held the bottle back a bit, wanting

her to reach for it, and he got just the show he wanted. As she reached, the tips of her breasts dipped into the steamy, swirling water. He imagined those tips in his mouth, and how he'd work those taut nipples with his tongue, his lips, his teeth.

And when she tipped the bottle to drink, he damn near salivated at the sight of her lips opening slightly, then tightening around the top of the bottle. She took a slow lingering drink.

Thunder grumbled overhead. The rain intensified to a pounding, as though battering its rage at the earth.

"These summer storms can get wild," Blaine murmured, setting the bottle on the edge of the tub. "Like a beast chained indoors for too long and suddenly released. Wonder when its full power will hit?"

And as soon as Blaine had said it, she also wondered when the truth of their connection—which seemed to constantly hover in the distance—would hit. Last night, they were no more than a hazy dream.

Tonight, their connection was sharper, more intense, yet still it seemed distant...as though waiting...

Donovan glanced over at Blaine, trying to decipher the look on her face in the muted light. He could see her silhouette—the soft curve of her cheek, the determined angle of her jaw—but he couldn't read more beyond that. He was still mulling over what she'd said, turning the words this way and that to better understand them.

Like a beast chained indoors for too long and suddenly released.

Wonder when its full power will hit?

Her questions had an edge, like a knife that sliced deep. He thought back to the pocketknife he kept on his bookshelf. In a funny way, it reminded him of Blaine. Small, rough on the outside, but sharp as hell on the inside.

"Have I said something to upset you?" Blaine asked quietly, interrupting his internal thoughts.

Yes, he wanted to say. *Just being here, just caring for you is a problem. I'm the beast who's been chained indoors too long. And I keep wondering when what we're doing will make sense, when the full power of it will hit.*

He'd avoided such encounters for this very reason.

But instead of voicing any of the thoughts raging through him, he answered simply, "I have a problem with boundaries."

"I know," she answered softly. "Although it hasn't seemed too much of a problem tonight, so far."

He'd never let her know what almost happened in the truck. How he'd almost let his boundaries encroach, corner him forevermore. Instead of providing a sanctuary, they almost became a prison.

He was so damn glad he'd realized that.

For a brief moment, he wondered if the storm he felt inside wasn't such a bad thing, after all.

"Sorry," he murmured.

"For what?"

"For being such a sullen bastard sometimes."

She made a sound like a suppressed giggle. "Well, earlier, I must admit you added to the room's moody ambiance."

He looked around at the shadows, the red-tinged

furniture, the hazy crimson glow. He couldn't help but laugh, too. "Yeah, this place belongs in an Edgar Allen Poe story, doesn't it?"

"And to think they call this Parisian Fantasy."

"With all the red, should be called the Telltale Heart."

She made a shuddering sound. "Great. We're miles from civilization in a strange little motel. A wicked storm is approaching. And we're on the verge of scaring the crapola out of each other by swapping scary tales."

"Great use of the room, eh?"

"Definitely different than what most people use it for, I'm sure. Telling Poe stories. Next we'll be spooking each other with our favorite Stephen King tales."

"Poe. King. What else could we share?"

He sensed her movement in the pool. The shift of her body as she moved closer. He closed his eyes and inhaled her scent, her heat.

Then he felt her lips. Almost hesitant as she kissed him, her mouth pressed lightly against his. She emitted a small, needy groan, as though this light, almost-nothing kiss was more than she could bear.

He leaned forward, wanting more...

Nothing.

He opened his eyes. She'd moved slightly to the left, out of his reach. Red light cascaded over her, giving her skin a smoldering luminescence. And in the light he caught her sassy, unrepentant smile.

"Teasing me, are you?" he asked huskily.

Her smile widened as she moved forward, the water splashing lightly with her movements.

Then he felt her body—hot, slick, wet—pressed against his, her full breasts flattened against his chest. She leaned close, so close he thought she was going to kiss him again. But instead her lips slid past his mouth. She pressed her soft cheek against his and whispered, her breath hot in his ear, "Teasing you? Mercilessly, I hope."

His fingers tangled into her hair and he pulled her face to his. So close, he saw how moisture beaded her upper lip. He gently rubbed his thumb across her lip, memorizing her mouth's cushiony texture. Damn, her Kewpie doll lips were so achingly soft, so kissable...

Take it slow, he reminded himself. Slow. Slow.

She licked her tongue along her bottom lip.

Slow.

Then she licked his thumb. First a little flick with the tip of her tongue. Then she ran it along his thumb's entire length, sensuously circling the thumbnail, then flicking her tongue all the way back down to the sensitive indentation of skin between his thumb and forefinger.

He growled deep in his throat.

Slow.

Her mouth continued to do naughty things with his thumb, kissing and licking and nibbling...and then she wrapped her lips around it and drew it deep into her hot, velvety mouth. And sucked it, hard.

Oh yeah, she was teasing him mercilessly all right.

His stomach muscles lurched.

Breath exploded from his lungs.

To hell with slow.

He wasn't sure what happened next, or who grabbed whom, but suddenly their bodies were intertwined in a viselike grip of thrashing and groaning, damp limbs, splashing water and hot kisses filled with even hotter, sweeter flavors. He finally anchored her head in place with both his hands, then meshed his lips to hers.

"Open for me, baby," he whispered at the corner of her mouth. "Open wide."

She parted her lips, then groaned out loud as his tongue penetrated her mouth. The water swirled around them like the hot, drizzly sexual feelings they were exploring. Silky hair twisted around his fingers. The faint scent of almonds tormented him. He moved his head, kissing her at a new angle, driving his tongue deeper. She moaned low in her throat. Her fingers dug into his shoulders as though holding on for dear life.

Lightning crackled with a searing sexuality.

Thunder crashed.

Their tongues tangled with a desperation that bordered on maniacal.

They pulled apart for a moment, both gasping.

"God, don't stop!" she yelled.

And they were all over each other again. Hands slipping over wet skin. Water frothing between them. Fingers sliding into crevices, massaging curves, pressing points of pleasure so exquisite they were like one writhing mass of frenetic desire.

Finally, he ripped himself away, his breath heaving.

"Slow," he croaked, feeling like a damn liar after that lusty explosion.

"No," she whimpered, reaching under the water and brushing her fingers along his testicles.

He grabbed her teasing hand and interlaced his fingers with hers.

He gulped air, trying to suck in enough to speak. "Slow," he repeated, fighting to catch his breath, "because...I want you...to be first."

Her mouth was open, panting. She frowned. "First?"

"First." He groaned, the sound guttural and desperate. "Blaine, honey..." He had to pause again to catch his breath. This slow stuff was killing him. "You never put yourself first, and by damn, tonight you will. Even if I have to force you."

She stared up at him with burning eyes.

He disengaged his interlaced fingers from hers and reached under the water. Finding her leg, he trailed his fingers along its sleek, wet skin...all the way up the shapely calf, over the firm thigh, then skirted the soft triangle of her sex.

"Sweet," he murmured, playing with the curls, which were lush and silky under the water.

Then he pressed his palm on her mound, not too hard, just enough to apply some pressure. Then he pulsed his hand with quick, fast motions.

Little mewing sounds escaped her throat.

He stopped.

Licking her lips, she thrust forward her pelvis under the water.

"More?" he asked.

"Oh, yes."

He felt along the side of the tub. There. A jet shooting water. Just the right amount of pressure.

"Come here." He pulled her body over to the jet and positioned her sweet cleft directly in the flow of shooting water.

"Ooooo!" She arched slightly, holding on to the side of the tub for support.

A hot ache coiled deep within him. Damn, he was so hard. Wanted her so bad.

But she was going to be first.

He positioned himself behind her and probed the tip of his erection between her thighs. Then he pushed, slowly, relishing the taut pressure of her slick, muscled legs encasing him.

He wanted just a taste. Nothing more.

He withdrew his member and, reaching around her, slid his fingers down her smooth tummy to the triangle of curls swirling in the rush of jetted water. He played around the periphery of that downy patch, then slipped a finger between her silky feminine folds, searching for that spot of pleasure.

"There?" he murmured into her ear, letting his warm breath tickle that soft, sensitive spot behind her ear.

"A little to the left."

He moved his finger.

She whimpered needily. "Oh...yes-s-s..."

"Lean back," he whispered gruffly.

"I...I don't think...I bend...that way."

He grinned. "I didn't say fold in two, I said lean back a little."

She did as told, leaning back until the back of her head rested on his shoulder. The position shoved her breasts high, the nipples pebbled and dark pink in the muted light.

"So damn beautiful," he murmured. With his free hand, he brushed one hardened bud, then the other. When she groaned, arching her back even more, he rolled one rigid nipple between his thumb and forefinger, then tugged it lightly.

Her breaths came rapidly. She writhed her hips against the pressure of the water combined with his finger, which was still manipulating her, building in intensity. Her breasts rose eagerly to the touch of his other hand as he continued stroking, squeezing, pinching their hard tips.

Her thighs trembled.

She thrust her hips in tandem with the increasing rhythm of his massaging finger.

With a soft shriek, she suddenly whirled, grabbed his head and forced it onto a breast. He pushed her against the side of the tub until he felt she had support, then he greedily clamped his lips around the tight bud, suckling it, drawing it fully into his mouth.

"I'm...so...close..."

He kept his finger on her nub, massaging it furiously, as he sucked and nipped at her full, needy breasts.

Thunder roared so loud, it rattled the windows.

Blaine groaned, calling his name.

He pulled back his head long enough to say, "Tell me what you want, Blaine. Put yourself first."

She started to speak, but instead grabbed his head and kissed him, fast and hard, devouring him as though she'd never tasted a male before in her life. Then she leaned back, heaved a huge intake of air, and said on a release of breath, "Just...keep...your...hand...there..."

Sensations throbbed through her, clamoring for release. Never in her life had she experienced feelings like this. Maybe she'd known passion before, but that was like hopping over a rock.

This damn, glorious experience was like climbing Pikes Peak.

She began rotating her hips as he manipulated her, spreading her legs to better experience the power of his oh-so-skilled touch.

"God," he murmured, "when you put yourself first—"

She thrust forward her breasts again, but pulled back just as his lips touched them. He groaned like an animal and flashed her a look that bordered on just plain sinful.

"Hey," he murmured, his open mouth still seeking her nipple. "No fair—"

"Hey," she whispered back huskily, "ladies first."

It was delicious and decadent to be so in control.

To be first.

She massaged both her breasts, watching him watching her, rotating and sliding her hips faster along his hand as hot, liquid sensations pooled in her groin.

Tension spiraled within her, tighter and tighter. Undulating, panting, she arched her back and wrapped her arms around his neck for support. "Don't...stop..."

The first wave of release crashed through her, shattering all awareness of anything other than the wonder of his rough hands massaging, stroking, kneading her. As rolling waves of release followed, she pressed forward, dipping the tip of one breast, then the other, into his mouth.

Intense satisfaction emanated from her groin, her nipples. She backed up slightly and felt the hot shooting water from the jet on her bottom. Oh yeah, she was putting herself first. Filling and giving herself every sensation she could stand.

When the desperate urgency finally subsided, she sank back into the water, falling into a sitting position on an underwater ledge. Air from the overhead fan cooled the slick sweat on her face, chest.

And for a long moment, they simply sat across from each other in the hot tub, staring each other down.

Finally, she wetted her lips and whispered hoarsely, "I like 'ladies first.'"

He nodded, a strand of wet hair dangling over his brow. "Me, too."

She stared at his brown eyes, the pupils large and dark. She'd felt his arousal...it thrilled her to know it was still there, ready and waiting. Oh, so patiently waiting. Damn, she'd never had a man put her needs first like that. Hold off on his own, making hers more important. She was accustomed to winging it in sex, hoping the by-product of a quick thrashing about might include a little orgasm for herself.

She never dreamed a woman could be on a pedestal, the star of the sex show.

It felt so good, so giving, she didn't know whether to laugh or cry. By forcing her to put herself first, Donovan had given her the gift of her own sexuality.

Given her the gift, in a sense, to be herself. To be a woman, desirable and deserving.

"You okay?" he finally said, breaking the silence.

"You kidding?" She leaned back and smiled. Water bubbled around her, its gurgling sounds mimicking her happiness.

Then she looked back down at Donovan. "Ladies first," she whispered, "means gentlemen second."

9

"GENTLEMEN SECOND?" Donovan's smile grew broader. "I'll second that."

He sat across the hot tub from her, damp strands of hair curling down his brow and neck, those brown eyes boring into her. His arms were propped on either side of him along the edge of the hot tub, that massive chest dark and glistening with drops of water and sweat.

He was ready, primed.

And waiting.

I'll second that. He'd just volleyed the ball into her court, but Blaine was unsure what move to use. Slam it back? Spike it?

Maybe just give it a touch, hard enough to return it, but light enough so he'd have to lunge for it.

But, unfortunately, this wasn't a sport she excelled at. This man-woman thing. Well, more specifically, this *subtle* part of the man-woman thing. Button-popping, hey, no prob! But this intricate, restrained, coy back-and-forth thing was too much like the courting ritual.

God, she wished she just knew the rules, then she'd know how to play this game. After all, rules were what made the world go around. Well, in Blaine's world anyway.

In the past, she'd tried to glean some of these convoluted man-woman courting-type rules by reading various "relationship books" her sister, Sonja, foisted on her. Probably because Blaine's courting style was to tackle dating like some kind of Olympic event.

So to appease her sister's concern, and because Blaine secretly hoped she'd learn some of these mysterious rules, she'd dutifully read a few of the books.

One discussed courting by stages, which looked great on paper but were damn confusing in real life. It talked about a "pursuit" stage, with words like "track," "hook" and "equipment" and made Blaine think it might be a better hunting guide than a relationship one.

Then there was the book that talked about finding Mr. Right as though it were a race. And which Blaine could have excelled at if the requirements involved sprinting or jogging, but no, the requirements involved things like buying perfume and lacy lingerie, which was like asking Blaine to visit an alien planet.

Finally she gave up on these books altogether when she read one that listed the top ten types of guys to avoid, which depressed her—and Blaine rarely got depressed—because it was like reading a list of all the guys she'd ever dated. Don't date a guy who's recently divorced, don't date a guy who drinks more than three beers a day, don't, don't, don't.

Except Donovan.

He wasn't on that list.

He was a stand-up guy. Strange decorating taste,

and a bit on the moody side, but what Sonja and her pals would call a "keeper." Decent, forthright, caring.

And one hell of a lover.

Plus, it was amazing to know someone less than twenty-four hours and discover things about yourself.

Like how good it feels to have your needs placed first. Or to feel special and beautiful and sensuous.

And now that they were playing "gentlemen second," she wanted to be good for him, too. He'd given her the thrill of a lifetime, made her body one melt-down-hot orgasm machine, and more than anything, she wanted to do something equally pleasurable for him.

Her heart pounded erratically.

God, like what?

"Blaine?" he asked.

"Yes?"

"You're frowning."

"I am?"

"You worrying about the bed?"

"The what?"

"The brass bed. Your sister's wedding gift."

"Right. The bed." She sighed heavily. "No, I wasn't worrying about that, but maybe I will. Give the other worry a break."

He chuckled. "I have a better proposition. Don't worry about *anything*." He paused. "Do you like old movies?"

"Like *Star Wars*?" Her roommate played those videos so much, she'd started calling him Luke.

"Older. Like *To Have and Have Not*. Bogie and Bacall."

She had to think for a moment. Oh yeah, Humphrey Bogart and Lauren Bacall. "I watched it on TV with my dad a few years ago."

"Well, do you remember Bacall saying to Bogie, 'You don't have to act with me? You don't have to say anything and you don't have to do anything'?"

Donovan remembered lines of dialogue from an old movie? She knew people's words carried great weight with him, but this was astounding. Blaine hoped he hadn't memorized every goofy thing she'd said, too.

"After Bacall told Bogie he didn't have to do anything," Donovan continued, "she said except maybe whistle. 'You know how to whistle, don't you?'" Donovan quoted, "'You just put your lips together and blow.'"

"You have an awesome memory." God, what goofy things had she said?

"A good memory has its pluses and minuses. Anyway, remembering that movie is easy. It's my mom's favorite. I must have watched it with her at least ten times the year I was holed up in my room, convalescing."

"Convalescing—?"

"What I was getting at," he continued, "is you don't have to worry about anything because, with me, you don't have to say anything or do anything. Just be you."

He'd ignored her unfinished question. And it was a big question. To spend a year of convalescence meant he'd had an illness. Or maybe been hurt? But she knew better than to ask anything. By not responding to her question, he'd put up the Do Not Enter sign again.

"Too bad I don't know how to whistle," she said, returning to their conversation.

"Come on." He cocked his head. "A sportster like you?"

"Nope. Never knew how. I used one of those metal whistles if I needed to. Otherwise, I yelled."

"Well, we'll work on your whistling," he said, his voice husky, suggestive. "Seems all you have to do is put your lips together and blow..."

Heat rushed through her. Good God Almighty this man revved her motor faster than a NASCAR driver.

The patter of rain, soft and incessant against the roof, faded into the background as her heart, beating wildly like some kind of pagan drum, came to the forefront. So loud, so frenetic, she swore Donovan had to hear it as well.

She glided her feet a little toward him, wondering if that was steam rising off the tub or the foggy haze of her aroused state.

She'd worried before about what move to use. Well, as Donovan had suggested, she'd can the worrying and just be herself. Forget all that coy stuff. Right now, her best move was to slide herself around this slick tub and take the man. Plaster her steamy, needy body against his hard, deserving one and roar to the finish line.

Donovan started to get out of the tub.

"Hey!" She lunged toward him, thinking to stop

him, but her feet slipped along the bottom of the hot tub. She lost her balance. Her arms flailed. After some thrashing about, during which she managed to totally submerge her head, she regained her footing.

And some of her dignity.

Sitting precariously again on her underwater ledge, she gasped a lungful of air, then managed to croak, "Where are you going?"

In the following moment of silence, she reminded herself that her honest, exuberant approach to life could be viewed as an attribute under certain conditions.

Maybe not this one, but certainly other conditions.

Donovan grinned. "With all your athletic skills, I'd assumed you knew how to swim, too."

She wiped the excess water out of her eyes. "I do," she said, hearing the defensiveness in her voice. "In regular-size pools, not itsy-bitsy hot tubs." She coughed, still recovering from that impromptu dunking. "Besides," she continued, "I wasn't swimming, I was lunging."

"At—?"

"You." The book that discussed the "pursuit" stage should have a special chapter dedicated to Blaine Saunders's unique tactics.

He chuckled. "I'm flattered. I've never been, uh, lunged at before by such a beautiful woman. I loved it."

Loved it? Her heart swelled with more than a little gratitude.

"I'm leaving to get a towel," he explained. "Be back in a minute."

He was so cool, so smooth, so...

So damn hot.

She salivated watching his wet, naked body emerge from the water. He'd gotten in the tub so quickly after he'd undressed, then they'd spent so much time in the water, she hadn't really gotten a good, solid look at his naked scrumptiousness until this moment.

Well, she did this morning, but they were both a bit stressed. Difficult to check someone out when you're furious, groggy and not sure what the hell happened.

But now she could check him out. Oh, yeah, and she'd enjoy every single moment.

He walked toward the bathroom, his body a red-glazed sinewy mass of man. A shadowy line ran the length of his back, couched on either side by sleek muscles. And below that, a butt that should be in a calendar. Hard, round...and even in this light, she saw the deep indentations of dimples on each cheek.

Dimples?

Be still my beating libido.

As he disappeared into the bathroom, she took several deep breaths, trying to calm down enough so when he returned she could appear in control.

Well, moderately in control.

Anyway, it wasn't her fault. Her sex drive had swerved off the road after his "put your lips together and blow" line.

She was practicing shaping her lips into a little O as he stepped out of the bathroom, one white towel draped over his broad shoulders, another towel in his hand. He walked toward the bed, tossed the towel he was holding on to it, then pulled the other towel across his back and started drying himself off.

Okay, okay, maybe the light was good enough to see killer dimples, but she was missing some major stuff in this moody Telltale Heart ambiance glow.

"It's too dark in here," she announced.

He stopped drying off a muscled bicep. "What?"

"Too dark," she repeated, waving around the room. "Can't see."

"Earlier you told me there was too much light—and now it's too dark?"

She shrugged. "I'm fickle like that. Off, on. Dark, light. Can never make up my mind."

He chuckled. "Right. Like I could believe that for a millisecond. Did I mention I have a bridge to sell you?" He stepped toward the shapely red lamp on the nightstand. "Maybe this has multiple settings. You know, low, medium, high."

She prayed for high.

He twisted a knob on the base of the lamp. The glow increased. He twisted again. The light diminished. "Appears to have only two settings," he murmured, turning it again to the higher one.

He looked at Blaine. "Better?"

The heightened illumination burnished his naked muscled body with a ruddy glow. "Much better," she whispered. "Much."

"Need more?"

"Oh, yeah." She grinned mischievously. "Don't need more light, though."

He did a double take. "You animal," he murmured.

"Grrrr. Now do me a favor and stay put. Let me enjoy the view."

Her gaze wandered greedily over his body, not sure where to begin. It was like staring up at the majesty of Pikes Peak with its primitive beauty and chiseled peaks and wondering where to focus a camera.

She focused on his face first. They'd shared many looks and glances, but she'd never felt invited to simply gaze into his eyes and look into the soul of the man.

Yet when she fixed her eyes on his, she felt both thrilled and frightened. And then it hit her. She was stepping over his strictest boundary, the invisible wall he built around him. A man didn't construct such a barrier if he didn't need to defend something.

As though he was resisting the intruder, his eyes narrowed. For a fleeting moment, there was nothing kind in his slitted gaze and she saw how Donovan might be cruel and domineering if he gave in to his dark side.

His lids opened wider again, the dark pools shifting to a liquid amber.

Just as she'd seen his darkness, she suddenly saw his radiance. And it was with awe that she looked into his face, the way it feels to catch the brilliance of the sun after a dark cloud has passed over it. This other side of Donovan, the part of him he hid so deeply, was *vulnerable*.

The truth rocked through her. *Something, someone has profoundly hurt him.*

A woman? She doubted that. Most guys who'd gone to war with the opposite sex acted like lions with inoperable thorns in their paws. Growling their dissatisfaction about women every chance they got.

No, it hadn't been a woman who'd hurt Donovan. It had been something else. Something that had shaken his world to its very core.

Maybe something related to that year of convalescence?

In the distance, thunder rumbled.

Blaine looked toward the window with its splinter of light where the drapes didn't quite close. "The storm is uncertain," she said quietly.

"Yes, keeps hinting that it's going to rage right on top of us any moment."

"And reveal itself," she murmured. Just like that flash of truth she'd seen in his eyes.

Wanting more than ever to make love, to quell whatever pain he held in his heart, she looked again at his body, amazed at the defined muscles in his chest, the taut ridged midriff, the chiseled lines of his thighs.

She swirled her hands in the water, eager to run her fingers over his hard, warm body again. "You're in awesome shape."

Donovan chuckled. "Awesome memory *and* body?" He gave his head a shake. "Blaine, you sweet talker you."

She stared at his chest, enjoying how the red light

played with the mass of chest hair, exposing wicked glints of red and gold.

Speaking of wicked...

She lowered her gaze and stared at his member.

Swollen, erect, just waiting for her...and if she lifted herself just a little, she could treat his deliciously hardened sex the way she'd treated his thumb a few minutes ago.

She raised herself and leaned toward him...

Donovan stepped back. "No," he said huskily. "Remember, it's gentlemen's choice."

She slipped back into the water. "I thought it was gentlemen second."

He chuckled again. "Same thing." He picked up a towel and held it open. "And this gentleman's choice is for you to get out of the tub."

Oooo, okay. *Now* things were getting good again.

She scooted her feet underneath her bottom until the soles were on the ledge she'd been sitting on, then she cautiously stood. No way she was going to risk toppling over and thrashing about again.

"Over here," instructed Donovan, indicating the spot next to the lamp with a nod of his head.

She stepped out of the hot tub, the lamp making the steam rising from her body a hazy red. She moved to the spot Donovan had indicated and stood.

He gazed boldly at her naked body, then raised the towel, inviting her into its folds. "You have an awesome body yourself."

"Some guy just told me I was beautiful, too."

"Who?"

Did he sound jealous? It gave her a delicious little thrill that Donovan might feel possessive of her.

"You," she answered softly.

He made a sound of appreciation as he wrapped the big, soft towel around her and began rubbing her dry. "Now *I'm* speaking the truth, so listen up." He gently massaged the towel along her arms and over the top of her chest. "You are a very beautiful woman, Blaine. A real treasure."

Blaine Saunders, a treasure? He was talking to her as though she were the gold at the end of the rainbow. She'd never been spoken to like this. Made to feel as though what she offered was sacred. Her heart soared and for a moment, the briefest of moments, she imagined loving this man for the rest of her life.

He carefully stroked the towel around her breasts, taking extra special care to ensure there wasn't even a single drop of water left between, under, or on top of each globe. "How am I doing?"

"Great," she croaked.

"You mentioned before that you'd like me to dab you dry, the way I had your tears."

He was treating her as though everything she said, even a passing comment, was important. "Thank you," she whispered.

He moved the towel across her tummy, brushing it dry. Next, he crouched down and caressed each leg with the towel, patting her down as though she were so fragile, so precious, that she might break her if he applied too much pressure.

"Turn around," he said.

She nearly spun a one-eighty.

"Not so fast."

"Sorry," she murmured.

And as Donovan drew the towel down her back, stroking her buttocks, then drying the back of each leg, she held back the tears of gratitude that threatened her already seriously shaky composure. She'd mused before about telling Sonja about this wild escapade at the Blazing Saddles Motel, but now Blaine realized that this was far more than a wild escapade.

She was being made love to.

No, Blaine could never tell Sonja about this because it was too precious. It was a gift Blaine would hold forevermore in her heart, in a secret place that was hers and hers alone.

"Turn around."

She did, slowly, hoping Donovan didn't see that she was trembling. Not from fear, but from the anticipation of too much love. Was that possible? To be given so much, to feel so cherished, that your body reacted as though terrified?

Donovan tossed the towel over a chair as he glanced up at the gauzy material that hung decoratively across the brass posters of the bed. He touched it. "Soft," he murmured. Then he pulled the gauzy strip off the posters, bringing it to his face. "Smells clean, fresh."

He pulled the strip of filmy material, which looked to be about six or seven feet long, three wide, and draped it around Blaine as though it were a luxurious fur wrap.

Then he stood back.

"Look at you," he said huskily. "Lady Godiva, watch out."

Blaine felt heat go to her cheeks.

"Am I embarrassing you?"

"A little," she confessed. "I'm used to being a tomboy, not a..."

"Delectable, desirable love goddess?"

Whoa, this guy could sling words better than a poet. "Something like that," she said softly.

Donovan turned to the bed and rolled over on top of it. But not before Blaine noticed the extra caution he took with one leg. The leg that he'd rubbed.

Donovan lay on his back, his hands behind his head. "Gentleman's choice," he reminded her in a low, forceful voice. "Stand at the foot of the bed, Blaine."

She did, clutching the gauzy fabric around her.

Donovan nestled back, savoring the sight of her standing there, so lusciously naked, draped in that see-through material. With the shades of red light in the room, and that floating white fabric, she looked like a portrait of innocence and sin.

He caught a look on her face and felt a pang of regret. "You're uncomfortable."

She blinked. "I, uh, never stood naked like this at the foot of a bed." She shifted from one foot to the other, gripping the fabric around her.

"Then don't." He patted the bed next to him. "Come lie down, listen to the rain with me."

She stopped shuffling her feet and stared him down. "No, I want to be gentleman's choice." She raised her chin a notch.

He had to bite his tongue to not smile. Damn, she was bullheaded...determined to win at sports *and* love-making. He settled back onto the lumpy mattress, relishing her eagerness.

"Let's make it a bit more comfortable, then," he suggested, turning slightly to fiddle with the radio on a table at the far side of the bed. Next to it were some small boxes he'd checked when he first came into the room. One was filled with condoms.

He found the power switch on the radio, then toyed with the dial. There was a lot of static as he searched for a station.

"Old radio," he said. "I remember my dad having one like this..." Donovan's mother still had that radio, a virtual antique, as well as other things of his father's. Donovan hadn't wanted anything, except what had been in his father's pockets when he died. His mother had thought it a crazy request, but it was meaningful to Donovan because after all his father's secrets, Donovan wanted to know the secrets his old man literally held the last day of his life.

And he'd gotten the pocketknife. Old, chipped, but still sharp. *Just like the old man, only he misused his edge.* He used it for his schemes, which cut deep, nearly ripping apart everything the family held dear.

A tune came in, clear and melodic. "Here we go," Donovan said, pleased he'd found music. "Too bad it's not the blues, though."

"I beg your pardon. You want some I'm-so-down-ain't-never-gonna-see-up-again song at a time like this?"

Donovan rolled over onto his back again, lacing his fingers behind his head. "Don't take it wrong, honey, I just love the blues. Besides, not all those songs are down-and-outers. Some are bottom-out sexy. Songs men—sometimes women—wrote because they were so head-over-heels hot for some luscious babe." He was getting a hard-on again just thinking how head-over-heels hot he felt for Blaine right now.

She noticed, too. Her smile took on that sassy edge he'd noticed in the hot tub and he grinned. God, he loved that smile. Like the Cheshire cat. So full of sex and fun.

Other men who hadn't made her feel special were damn fools.

She gyrated her hips a little, swaying in time to the music. "Oh, Chris Isaak," she whispered. "I love this song."

Donovan rarely listened to popular music, but this Isaak fellow could hold his own in the blues world if he wanted. His voice was melodic, soulful, and damn if he wasn't crooning about wanting a woman so bad it hurt.

Oh, yeah, this song would work just fine. Bluesy and sexy.

Blaine had picked up the mood, too, as she began dancing a little, sashaying back and forth, holding the gauzy material around her.

A pop of fluorescence.

Lightning.

And in that moment, Donovan had an image of Blaine in white, dancing at a wedding.

Blaine, his bride.

Thunder rumbled, shaking apart the image.

Shaking apart Donovan's thoughts, which scattered in his mind as though they had feet. Running from the image of "ever after"—the *last* thing he wanted in his life.

He started to shift, to turn off the radio, to suggest that they call if a night, just use the room to rest and sleep and head out tomorrow once the coast was clear.

But damn if Blaine didn't pull a fast one.

She began doing a slow, exotic striptease with that strip of nothing material.

Donovan couldn't move. Watching Blaine go all-out sex-siren was like being injected with pure lust. His body on fire, he watched as she drew the gauzy material around her, exposing parts of her body, then sensuously covering them again.

Teasing him mercilessly.

He surged forward and grabbed her, gauze and all, and positioned her over him, on her knees.

"One moment, baby." He reached for the box, flicked open the lid, and extracted a small foil wrapper. Ripping it open, he quickly unrolled it onto his hard shaft.

Then he leaned back. "Ride me, Blaine."

She eased herself onto the tip of his sex and rotated her hips slowly around his hardened ridge.

He growled deep in his throat.

She stared boldly into his eyes and licked her lips.

Pulling up her knees, she slid, slowly, ever so slowly, down his member and began rocking back and forth.

He glanced from her to the mirror overhead, relishing the double view of her movements. Above, he caught flashes of her flexed thighs and jutting breasts as she moved.

But even better was the view when he looked straight ahead. Blaine's desirous expression, the gleam in her eyes. If it was a turn-on to be appreciated, it was a fiery aphrodisiac to be coveted.

Waves of heat blasted through him.

He groaned and grabbed her hips, increasing the rhythm of her movements, pressing deeper into her.

She whimpered, opening her legs wider to accommodate the full length of his shaft.

With a guttural groan, he thrust deep, filling her completely.

She emitted a faint cry, paused, then slammed herself on top of him.

He met her thrusts with his own, meeting her sweetly brazen gaze. She was wild, her passion unleashed. Her desire strong, electrifying.

Arching her back, she whimpered. She thrust forward her breasts, the nipples hard with need.

He grabbed her swollen mounds and kneaded them, rolling the distended buds between his fingers, eyeing the overhead mirror and the image of her face as she arched her back, eyes closed, panting. The gauzy strip of material partially clung to the sweat on her body, the rest floated behind her. Her nails dug into his chest. She rode him like a beast that needed to be tamed.

He gritted his teeth against the fierce need to come,

but even in his fever-soaked state, damn it, he wanted her to...

Her insides clamped tight around him.

"I'm...I'm..."

"Give it to me, Blaine, honey," he growled, raising his hips to penetrate her as deep as she'd take it.

She cried out, a sound filled with agony and pleasure. Her insides convulsed wildly.

He damn near shot off the bed as he slammed into her, harder and harder, his movements rising with her cries.

And then, for a moment, the world coalesced into a ball of white-hot need before he exploded into her. He pulled her tight against him, shoving himself into her as release—sweet, hot release—roared through him.

Afterward, they lay sandwiched together, their bodies slick with sweat. He hugged her close, molding her against him, liking how she fit. She pressed against his boundaries in the most literal sense, but it didn't feel invasive.

It felt...*right*.

As though they'd joined in flesh and spirit.

10

DONOVAN BLINKED OPEN his eyes. A narrow stream of sunshine poured through a slit in heavy, red drapes. Cool ripples of air flowed over his skin. *Another motel room.* He rubbed his eyes and yawned. *Which town am I in?* Cincinnati? San José?

He slid a glance to the right. A hot tub.

God, yes, he remembered what city he was in...

Turning his head, he checked out the bed.

Empty.

He leaned up on one elbow and looked around the room.

Empty.

"Blaine?"

The only sound was the whirring of the overhead fan.

The door to the bathroom was open, but it was dark in there. No hiss of shower spray, or the taps and clicks a woman makes as she puts on makeup, fusses with her hair.

But Blaine didn't bring makeup. Or a purse. All she'd brought was herself and the clothes on her body.

Her clothes! He darted a gaze around the room, but they weren't anywhere.

She dressed and left?

With no car?

He checked out the clock radio. 8:00 a.m. Next to the radio, a fluttering piece of yellow paper caught his eye. He picked it up. Part of a yellow page ripped out of a phone book. Across the top were some scribbled words.

He rolled over, twisted the knob on the curvy red lamp, then stuck the paper under the arc of light and read.

"Dear Donovan, I used your cell phone to call a nearby car repair shop. They gave me a lift to Henry's truck. I didn't want to wake you. Blaine. P.S. Thank you for the tequila, food and the delicious opportunity to put my needs first."

He reread it several times, each time his eyes lingering on the "delicious opportunity" part.

She couldn't have waited? I'd have given her a lift to some damn car repair place.

She wanted out of here, fast.

It was the kind of note he might have written back in college, before sneaking out of some coed's room at the crack of dawn. Back then, he'd felt carefree, noncommittal.

This morning, he felt pissed.

Other emotions crowded in, like regret and disappointment, but he stuffed them back down. Worse, he didn't even know what he was reacting to. Had he offended her? Done something she didn't like?

Hell, maybe she'd decided last night was just a mistake. Maybe her joke about being fickle wasn't a joke after all.

His gut hurt as though he'd been sucker punched.

Maybe he felt so damn bad because he wanted more? He, the guy who closed out the world, suddenly felt a void?

Need coffee.

Hot, black.

Nothing like a jolt of caffeine to put the world back into focus. He crawled out of bed and headed to the automatic coffeemaker in the bathroom, although deep inside, he knew this didn't have a damn thing to do with gaining focus. If anything, Blaine had sharpened his view on life. Given him a taste of what could be.

Then ripped it all away.

He wadded Blaine's note into a ball and tossed it into the trash.

"WELL, HELLO STRANGER!" Blaine's dad, sitting at his desk, looked at her expectantly. He quickly tossed a napkin into the trash.

"Hello," Blaine said. She paused next to his desk and glanced at the trash can. "What were you eating?"

"Carrot..." He smiled sheepishly. "...cake."

"Dad," she said, a warning in her voice, "you're supposed to be on a diet." She sat down in her ergonomic chair and faced the sea of sticky notes. She really should break the habit of notes and learn to better use the computer.

"How can I stay focused on my diet when I'm worried about you?"

He got up and ambled over to her desk. Blaine caught the edge of a bright red wrapper sticking out of his shirt pocket. Looked suspiciously like the tip of a candy bar.

"Your sister has been calling about that bed..."

"It's in transit." She had to call Ralph, ask where his buddy—a Barry somebody—delivered it this time. But she didn't want to go into details about this lost bed saga with her dad. Not yet. "Have I missed any important maid-of-honor or other sisterly wedding tasks?"

"Nope, everything's under control. With everybody and their brother chipping in, we almost have too much help. Only thing you need to do is try on the gown Sonja picked out for you to wear. It's real pretty. She calls it 'jade' but I call it 'lagoon green.'"

"Just as long as it doesn't have puffy sleeves that look like water wings, I'm okay with whatever she picked." Blaine frowned. "I'm not doing enough for Sonja," she murmured. "A girl needs her mother and sister—both of which are now me—to help with all the bridal duties—"

"Sweetheart," her dad interrupted, "it's okay to take some time for yourself, too, you know. Besides, we're on volunteer overload... Henry wanted to play barbecue chef at the reception, and I had to turn him down." Her dad snapped his fingers. "Been so caught up in wedding stuff, I almost forgot! Henry's been calling about his truck. I tried phoning you, but your roommate said you were out all night."

She looked up into her dad's concerned expression. Biting the inside of her bottom lip, Blaine gathered her thoughts. She wanted to explain so he wouldn't worry—but that was why she hadn't wanted to talk about the bed. She wasn't sure herself what last night, or the night before, meant... Her heart and mind were inextricably coiled together like that brass beauty's headboard.

And similar to that intricate pattern, her feelings soared and dropped in all directions at once.

All because of Donovan.

"Henry's truck broke down outside of town," she began. "So I had to leave it on the side of the road. With the storm kicking up, I thought it best to just spend the night at, uh..."

Her father gasped. "At the Blazing Saddles Motel?"

She touched his arm. "Now, Dad, I was okay. Really. I couldn't call you because, uh, of the roaming."

"Roaming?"

"The cell phone I had access to couldn't get a signal to Manitou."

He frowned, looking out the window at Henry's pickup. "How'd you get help to fix the truck if the phone couldn't roam?"

"This morning, I called a car repair shop close to the motel. You know, within roaming distance. Fortunately, it was a fairly minor hose fix. Two hours later, I drove back here, showered and changed, and here I am."

She made it all sound so simple, never alluding there had been more, so much more. It was almost as though she'd packed a lifetime into the last few days...and maybe, she realized, there was a reason for that. You lived the moment to the fullest if that moment was temporary.

"Would you be a sweetie and call Henry again?" she continued. "Because he lives so close to the agency, I figured it was easiest to drive the truck here so he can pick it up whenever he'd like. Oh, and tell him I'm giving him an IOU for two days' free repair on anything in his house for any inconvenience I caused."

"Fine, sweetheart," her dad said. His worried look shifted to a questioning one. "How'd you pay for the repair?"

"The magic of credit cards." She'd be glad when business picked up. And when that bank loan was approved. "I'm running out of magic, though."

Br-ring. Br-ring.

"Maybe that's the bank!" She wrung her suddenly clammy hands.

"I'll get it," her father said, adopting his receptionist voice. "You take a moment and relax, pull your thoughts together." He picked up the receiver. "Welcome. This is the Blaine Saunders Agency. May I be of service?"

He paused, his eyes widening.

"Yes, may I tell her who's calling?"

"One moment, please." He pressed the mute button. "It's that fellow again!"

"What fellow?"

"The one who called before."

"Oh, no." Her stomach dropped. "Not David."

"No!" Her father looked as though he was going to burst. "That Donovan Roy fellow."

"Donovan?"

"Yes!"

He'd called yesterday. Now he was calling again. Her nerves notched higher. It was taking every ounce of her emotional stamina to accept whatever had happened between them was temporary—but if he kept calling, she'd have a hell of a time maintaining this acceptance.

"Are you two dating?" her father.

She shook her head no. What had happened wasn't exactly *dating*.

Before her father could ask another question, she waggled her fingers, indicating he was to hand over the phone. "I'm buying you some *Field and Stream* magazines," she muttered to her dad as she lifted the receiver to her mouth. "You and *Good Housekeeping* need a trial separation." She released the mute button.

"Hello?"

"Hello." Donovan's voice. Rich, deep.

She glanced at her father and pointed at his desk chair. "Go!" she mouthed. It was difficult enough having this morning-after conversation without her father hulking over her desk, matchmaker written all over him.

"You, uh, got my note?" Blaine asked, trying to sound professional.

Her father reluctantly inched back to his desk, his gaze glued on Blaine's face.

"Yes. Surprised you had to leave so early."

"You know me," she said, trying to sound light-hearted. She picked up her NASCAR racing car model. "Fast, fast, fast!"

There was a pause on the other end. "Is the truck getting fixed?"

"All done."

"You *are* fast." He paused. "Question."

She waited. "Yes?"

"Did I offend you last night?"

"No."

"Do something you didn't like?"

She slid a stop-listening look at her father, who began dusting off his bowling trophy. "No," she whispered.

"So is it true that you're fickle?"

Fickle? Then she recalled her silly comment last evening. Had he taken her seriously? "No," she whispered more emphatically.

"Can't talk?"

"Riiight," she said with relief. She started feeling that connection again with Donovan. A dangerous thing to feel with a temporary man.

"Sorry. Don't want to make you uncomfortable. Just a few more questions—none about last night. Did you call Ralph? Find out where his friend delivered the bed?"

"I just got in. That was first on my list." She lowered her voice. "You don't need to worry about that bed. This is my responsibility."

"I feel responsible, too, you know. Because of me, that bed is lost. I want to help."

She closed her eyes, not wanting Donovan's help. That meant seeing him again, connecting with him again.

"I did a little investigating on that bed," Donovan said.

Her eyes popped open. "You did?"

"Yes. I checked eBay on the off-chance someone might be trying to unload a hot bed. Fortunately, that's not the case, but I did find a photo of it."

She straightened in her seat. "Photo? Of my bed?"

"Yes. We only spent one night on it, but I remember everything about that bed."

A shiver went through Blaine as she recalled that first night, their dreamy lovemaking.

"Care to have lunch with me?" he asked.

"Lunch?"

She bit her lip. Too late. Her father was at her desk again, mouthing the word "lunch" as well. He looked so elated, she didn't have the heart to send him away again.

"And I don't mean fast food," Donovan said with a chuckle.

Lunch. Being near Donovan. Blood zinged through her body. Her pulse thundered in her ears. Damn him anyway. How could she be close and remain temporary?

"No," she whispered. "You can tell me about your investigation on the phone..."

Her father dropped his head into his hands.

"I'd much rather tell you in person," Donovan said. He dropped his voice. "You don't have to be strong by yourself all the time, Blaine. Let me help you."

No man had ever offered to support her like this. She felt the exhaustion of handling everything slip off her shoulders. Maybe this was the time to put herself first, accept help.

Plus, she missed him. Longed to see him again. She laid her damn "temporary" pride on the line. "Yes, lunch would be good," she murmured.

Her father feigned a "hurrah" pose, both hands raised over his head.

"I'll pick you up in ten minutes?" Donovan asked.

Blaine looked at the clock. Eleven-thirty. "Works for me."

"See you then."

"Hey," Blaine said, catching him before he hung up.

"Yes?"

"You know where I work, right?"

"Sure, *Blaze*," Donovan teased. "At some motel outside Manitou, right? See you in ten."

Before Blaine could say anything, Donovan hung up. Fighting a grin, she hung up her phone. For such a moody fellow, he could sure be a charmer when he wanted.

"So! You have a lunch date!" Her father's eyes gleamed.

"It's just *lunch*, Dad, not an engagement party."

"Let's get you gussied up," he announced, clapping his hands together.

Blaine shook her head. "Dad, he's going to be here in ten minutes. I'm about as gussied as I'm going to get." She looked down at her clean pair of jeans and her new T-shirt, suddenly wishing she could borrow one of Sonja's skirts or sundresses. "Wish I looked a bit prettier, though..."

"I'll run across the street to the supermarket and buy

some lipstick," her dad said, making a beeline for the door.

"Dad, no, that's not necessary—"

The door slammed shut behind him.

She squeezed shut her eyes, fighting the flurry of butterflies in her tummy. *I'll call Ralph. That'll get my mind off Donovan for a few minutes.*

Ralph wasn't home, so she left a message, knowing as soon as he heard the word "bed" he'd probably shoot his answering machine.

A few minutes after Blaine hung up, her dad marched back in, all business. "Picked up a loo-loo of a color. Cherry Coco Shimmer."

"Sounds like an exotic dancer." Blaine held up her hands in a "no way" gesture, but he ignored her, scrutinizing the lipstick in the light.

She paused, realizing this is just how he acted those years right after her mom died. He had wanted so much to help Blaine be feminine, to wear pretty dresses and new hairstyles and makeup like other teenage girls. She rarely gave in, mainly because it was just too much fuss. But now she realized how important it was for him, too. It was his way of being a dad *and* mom.

She glanced at the framed photo of the family on her desk. "You're loving this, aren't you?" Blaine whispered to her mom. "Your tomboy is getting a mini-beauty makeover."

Looking back at her dad, Blaine said, "Okay, Cherry Coco Shimmer, here we come!"

ALMOST TEN MINUTES LATER, Donovan strolled into the agency. Blaine felt momentarily paralyzed at the sight of him. He wore a pair of jeans—no rips—and a short-sleeved shirt the color of golden sand. The color complemented his tan, his rich brown mane, but especially that whiskey color in his eyes. His hair was brushed back and tied neatly at his neck in a small ponytail. Which better exposed his solid, angular face that had a strip of beard underneath his bottom lip.

He'd shaved. Sort of. Leaving that bold slash of beard was obviously calculated.

Her body shivered with pleasure.

Damn, Matthew McConaughey could only *wish* to look so good.

Blaine's father stood, walked around his desk, and stopped. Extending his hand, he said, "Douglas Saunders," in a very non-receptionist voice.

She held her breath. She'd made her father *swear* he wouldn't embarrass her by playing matchmaker...

"Donovan Roy," responded Donovan, shaking her father's hand.

The men stood back, not breaking eye contact.

Blaine quickly stood, eager to get out of here before her father succumbed to any not-so-subtle "I want Blaine married" antics. "Let's go!" she said, a bit too exuberantly.

Donovan looked over and did a double take.

Blaine smiled, then pursed her lips, remembering she had Cherry Coco Shimmer slicked all over her mouth.

"You look pretty." Donovan's eyes twinkled.

Blaine's father turned and smiled proudly. "Yes, doesn't she?"

Blaine marched up to Donovan and, for lack of what else to do, patted him on his shoulder. "Okay, okay, let's go." She looked at her dad. "See you soon."

Uh-oh. Her dad's eyes were growing misty. "See you, sweetheart," he said in a shaky voice.

She steered Donovan toward the door. As Donovan held it open for her, she glanced over her shoulder.

Her father was holding up both hands, his fingers crossed.

FIFTEEN MINUTES LATER, Blaine and Donovan were sitting on the outside deck of the Stagecoach Steak and Ale restaurant.

Sun sifted through a canopy of cottonwood trees. Below the Fountain Creek gurgled. And thanks to her allergy medicine, she enjoyed the scent of roses from a nearby clay pot. Blaine had been to this restaurant before on special occasions. Her sister's graduation. Her dad's birthday.

But never on a date.

This isn't a date, she reminded herself for the umpteenth time while she wondered how her lipstick was behaving.

"What're you having?" Donovan asked.

Everything on the menu looked so fancy. Crab cakes. Lemon herb chicken. "All I really want is a cheeseburger and fries," she confessed.

"Me, too."

She closed the menu with a sigh of relief. "Thank God."

After the waiter took their order, Blaine turned her attention back to Donovan. A shaft of sunlight struck his head, burnishing gold on his dark locks. His skin was bronze from spending so much time outdoors. Lines splayed from the edges of his eyes and curved around his mouth. She could see in his face that life hadn't always been easy. Or maybe even fair. And yet she was struck with his confidence, and how it imbued him with a powerful authority.

If he didn't build so many barriers, he could rule the world.

He was powerful in other ways, too. Just sitting here, looking at him, caused her stomach to quiver and her palms to sweat. Arousal shot through her, weakening her, and she had the giddy sensation she stood at the top of an abyss, ready to fall...not unlike the feeling she'd had their first morning-after.

She drew in a shaky breath, immediately conscious that doing so drew attention to her breasts. She never wore a bra with T-shirts, and from the look on Donovan's face, he was well aware of that fact now.

And thanks to her pert nipples, well aware of the effect he had on her. She knew she shouldn't have come. She'd accepted an invitation to discuss the bed, not blast messages with her body like some humanoid Blazing Saddles neon sign.

Donovan tried not to stare, but only a blind man wouldn't notice two taut nipples peeking at him through a thin cotton shirt. Heated memories of kneading and suckling them raced through his mind.

He looked back up into her face and caught the embarrassed flush on her cheeks. A rosy pink, but not as pink as that luscious color on her lips. It made her full lips just that much more inviting. More memories seared his brain. His lips plundering hers. Their bodies writhing for control...and for release.

And here she sat across the table from him, blushing like a schoolgirl. He'd never had this experience before where a relationship started out with wild, unbridled sex and then progressed to sweet dates where they went out for burgers and fries.

Relationship? Had he just described what they were doing as a *relationship?*

As though on cue, the waiter reappeared. "Rare?" he asked, holding two plates.

"That's me," Donovan answered, his voice suddenly raspy. It would be a *very* rare thing for him to settle into a relationship. Years from now, maybe, after this whole ranch mess was settled. But not right now. Life was complicated enough.

After eating in silence for a few minutes, Donovan took a swig of his iced tea. He set down the glass, then swiped at a drop of moisture that ran down its side. It reminded him of drying off Blaine, rubbing drops of water off her naked body.

It had felt so damn good to see that look of sweet gratitude on her face.

And so damn bad this morning when he realized she'd left.

Maybe he didn't want a relationship, or didn't feel he could handle one right now, but he didn't want to be without her, either. For all the walls he'd so carefully built, he never dreamed he'd find himself sitting smack on the middle of one, torn, not knowing whether to protect himself or let his heart go free.

"I'm surprised you haven't asked what I unearthed on eBay yet," he said, steering his thoughts back to the reason why they were here.

She blinked and swallowed. "I didn't want to pry."

"But, I already mentioned it to you so you wouldn't be prying."

She was fingering a fry. "I'm, uh, trying to respect your privacy."

"Oh." Maybe that was a good thing. It would keep him in check, anyway.

"Well," he said, settling back in the patio chair. "As I said, I saw a picture of your bed on eBay. I'm ninety-nine percent certain it's your bed, anyway."

"You have an excellent memory, so I believe you."

When she listened intently, she had the most guileless look. Reminded him of when they'd woken up together and realized they were lovers. God, that moment had felt ecstatic, intense...like being struck by lightning.

Whoa, buddy, switch gears.

"And your bed has a legend attached to it," he said quickly, forcing himself to stay on the topic.

Her hand froze as she reached for another fry. *"Legend?"*

"Seems your bed has a history of legendary lovers.

Folklore says Napoleon and Josephine, Fitzgerald and Zelda, even Elizabeth Taylor and Richard Burton slept in it."

"Elizabeth Taylor?" Blaine's deliciously pink lips were open, her eyes wide.

"There's more. The bed, it appears, has a habit of disappearing and showing up in new, mysterious places."

She blinked. "Well, *that's* not folklore."

"But here's the best part. It's possibly worth ten to fifty times what you paid."

"Twenty or a *hundred* thousand?"

"Probably because of the lovers who slept in it. You know, like owning one of Mickey Mantle's rookie cards."

She sucked on the straw to her milk shake, wide-eyed and pensive. After swallowing, she continued, "Do you believe that legendary lovers story?"

Truth be told, no. But he didn't believe in a lot of things anymore. Except when he was with Blaine. Something about her wholesomeness and enthusiasm were rubbing off on him. Hell, he'd probably believe in Santa Claus again if he hung out with her long enough.

"Sort of," he finally answered. "Mainly because the bed has increased substantially in value."

Her eyebrows shot up. "I just thought of something," she whispered.

"What?"

"Gwyneth Paltrow is supposed to be in Colorado Springs this week, staying at that upscale Broadmoor hotel while promoting her newest film about star-crossed lovers." She smiled. "My dad read about it in, uh, one of his magazines."

Donovan wasn't ready for this U-turn. "Okay."

Blaine leaned over and whispered conspiratorially. "Maybe somebody knows the legend of the bed and *stole* it! Took it to The Broadmoor so Gwyneth could sleep in it...you know, add another legendary lover to the folklore."

"What's in that milk shake?"

"I'm serious."

"I know."

She glanced at her wristwatch. "It's almost one." She looked back up, her green eyes sparkling like sunlight on the sea. "We could make it to The Broadmoor by one-thirty."

"Why don't you just call Ralph and ask what his buddy did with the bed?"

"I will. On the way to The Broadmoor. If Ralph answers, and knows where the bed is, great! We'll forget about The Broadmoor. But if he doesn't answer, and there's a high probability of that 'cause he's fed up with both of us, it doesn't hurt to swing by the hotel."

He paused. "And what do we do when we get there? Ask which room Gwyneth Paltrow is staying in?"

And that's when he saw a look of near-desperation cloud Blaine's eyes. "The bed, it's..." She cleared her throat. "...it's so important. For Sonja," she added quickly.

For *you*, thought Donovan. And suddenly, it was important to him, enormously important, to do whatever it took to help Blaine get back that piece of magic in which she'd invested not only her money, but also her heart.

"Okay, but let's not get arrested for breaking or entering..."

She grinned, that mischievous, life-affirming smile that did funny things to his insides.

"Do you realize what's happening?" she asked, flagging down the waiter for the bill. "You, the rebel, are starting to worry about breaking rules...and me—the rule-follower—I'm starting to enjoy breaking them." Her smile widened. "We're good for each other!"

Uncertainty pierced his heart with a sharp ache. He wanted to believe, desperately, that maybe it was true. She'd been good for him, that was for certain. At a dark time in his life, Blaine had appeared like a beacon, showing him he could experience passion and joy.

But he wasn't so sure what he had to offer. Whatever it was, it couldn't be all that good. His baggage damn near smothered his own life—no guessing the damage it could do to someone else's. No, Blaine deserved something better. She deserved a man who could nurture her and support her...

And love her.

And when he looked into her shining face, with those eyes that twinkled with eagerness, he wished fervently he could be that man.

11

DONOVAN AND BLAINE walked across the white marble floor of The Broadmoor lobby and halted.

"If I could whistle, I would," whispered Blaine, trying not to gawk at the uniformed bellmen who scurried about like toy soldiers, the massive flower arrangements that infused the room with fragrances of lavender and roses, the multitiered chandelier that hung like a sparkling sun. "No wonder Gwyneth Paltrow stays here...this place is out of a Hollywood movie."

"You've never been here?" said Donovan.

"Are you kidding?"

"Not even with a prom date for dinner at one of their romantic restaurants?"

"No." She didn't want to admit she never even *went* to a prom. "Did you?"

"God, no. Back in high school, I never fit in with all that."

"Just like me," she murmured, realizing yet another connection they had. "And yet you wanted a trophy wife."

"And thank God, again, that I didn't end up with one."

Blaine met his gaze and for a crazy moment, she

wondered what it would be like to be called Donovan's wife.

Crazy, all right. They were here on a mission, not a fantasy.

"I'll go to the front desk and ask if a big brass bed was delivered here today," Blaine said.

A few minutes later, she returned. "They said they'd call facilities, but it started getting complicated when they asked who I was and why I needed to know...so I said I was just curious about the kinds of beds they had here and left."

"Blaine, think through whatever you say before you say it, deal? Let's not draw the wrong kind of attention to ourselves."

"I'll watch the blurting. Plan B," Blaine said, lowering her voice. "Gwyneth probably travels with a bodyguard or two, so keep your eyes peeled for anyone who has that Secret Service look. Wherever he's loitering has to be near Gwyneth's room."

Donovan dragged his hand through his hair. "This search is so random."

"So you said all the way out here. But you also said you wanted to help."

"And you agreed we'd only spend an hour or two here, tops."

"Yes, that's what we agreed." She didn't want to look at Donovan right now because she knew she'd see that incredulous look on his face again. The look that said even though he was on her side, this was the wackiest adventure he'd ever been roped into. But considering Ralph didn't answer her follow-up call, and she had no idea who his buddy "Barry" was, *and* discovering the bed had a "legendary lovers" folklore attached to it, checking out the location of a legendary lover like Gwyneth Paltrow didn't seem so odd.

Even if there were no other reasons, knowing the bed might be worth a hundred times what she paid, they could spare an hour or two on a search.

Blaine saw a buffed looking guy in a dark suit with a telephone-thingy stuck in his ear stroll purposefully across the lobby toward the wide, carpeted staircase.

"Let's go," she whispered, heading toward the staircase.

A few minutes later, she and Donovan stood at the top of the stairs on the second floor.

"Where'd he go?" Blaine looked around. She glanced up the stairs leading to the next level. "He didn't head up there."

"Let's take a moment to exercise caution, stop chasing men in black," muttered Donovan, looking over the banister at the milling people and the registration desk below. He stepped back so he couldn't be seen. "All we need is for some bodyguard type to catch us tailing him."

"Bet he entered one of the rooms on this floor," Blaine said, ignoring Donovan's comment, "which means we're in the right place."

A clattering sound drew their attention. They both turned and saw a plump housekeeper, attired in a smock that matched the color on the walls, steer a cart filled with towels, soaps and other items off a service elevator. She headed to a door and knocked. "House-keeping," she called out.

"Perfect," whispered Blaine, heading toward the housekeeper.

"What are you doing—?" he whispered in a strangled voice, reaching out to stop her, but catching only air.

As Blaine approached, the housekeeper smiled pleasantly. "May I help you?"

Blaine stood awkwardly next to the cart, digging her toe into the carpet. "Sure. Is Gwyneth Paltrow on this floor?"

The housekeeper's smile faded. Her eyebrows pressed together. "Gwyneth?"

"Gwyneth Paltrow, the movie star. Is she on this floor?"

Donovan winced, fighting images of him and Blaine sitting in a holding tank, explaining they really weren't stalking an actress, but a bed.

The housekeeper pulled a cell phone out of a pocket. *Great. She's calling hotel security.* Donovan quickly stepped up to the cart and smiled his best charming smile. "Darling," he said to Blaine, "did you get the soap?" He looked at the housekeeper. "We ran out of soap," he explained.

"Really?" she said, holding the phone. "Eh, what room you in?"

"Room...eight hundred," Blaine said.

The housekeeper waited a beat before responding. "We don't have a room eight hundred."

Donovan gripped Blaine by the elbow. "Darling, we're late for our tennis match." He tossed a smile at the housekeeper, debating whether to call her darling, too. "We'll get soap later. Thanks."

Out of the corner of his eye, Donovan saw the woman punch a number into the phone.

He damn near dragged Blaine down another hallway, out of view of the housekeeper. "Slick move, sleuth," he whispered into her ear. "She's reporting us to security."

"There's no exit down this hallway," Blaine said, stumbling alongside Donovan.

Donovan jerked his head forward. Ahead a hundred or so feet, the hallway terminated in a wall. He halted, releasing his grip on Blaine.

She jiggled a doorknob.

"*Now* what are you doing?" he whispered.

She lunged forward and jiggled another knob.

"Blaine," Donovan said in a warning voice.

She jiggled another. The door opened. She shot a look at him. "We'll hide from the posse in here."

"If we're caught in a room, that's worse than simply asking for soap—"

"Get in!" she whispered, ducking inside. Her hand shot back outside, motioning frantically.

More clattering.

He looked behind him. The edge of the cart rolled into view.

Donovan jumped inside the room.

Blaine, breathing hard, carefully shut the door with a soft click. "Can you believe it?" she whispered, her face flushed with excitement. "We're breaking rules again!"

He stepped into the room, away from the door. "No, *you're* breaking rules. I'm along to make sure we stay out of jail."

"See?" She followed him into the room. "I told you we're good for each other." She looked around. "Wow."

Wow was right. From the richly patterned wall-to-wall rug to the satiny fabric-covered walls to a bed that made king-size look puny. "At least you picked a room that no one's in," Donovan commented.

"We'll wait for the coast to clear, then make our grand escape."

He looked at the daredevil twinkle in her eyes and felt a grudging admiration. He thought he'd thumbed his nose at the world this past year? Blaine and her adventurous streak made him look like a damn amateur.

"Wow," Blaine said again, perusing the room. She gestured toward the polished mahogany desk covered with a leather-bound book, an antique brass horse and a crystal vase filled with exotic seashells. "This room has gobs of knickknacks." She looked at Donovan. "You know what a knickknack is, right?"

"I know what they are. I just don't own any."

"Well, except for that pocketknife and plant, but on second thought, I guess they don't qualify as knick-knacks."

It was weird to discuss his private world. Up until he'd found Blaine in his bed, no one, except Milly and some service people, had been in his place. A year ago, that's exactly the way he wanted it. His home wasn't just a castle, it was his fortress.

But listening to Blaine's teasing comments about how he lived, he felt oddly comforted to be *known*.

"The plant was a housewarming gift from Milly," he explained. "But the knife..." He paused, debating if this was a boundary he wanted to remove. And that's when he realized that among the things Blaine had resurrected with him, feeling safe was one of them. He could trust her. Damn, he hadn't trusted anyone in so long, the reaction was foreign. "The knife is all I have of my father's. It's what was in his pocket when he died."

She tilted her head, her face filled with silent questions.

"It represents what he did and what I never want to be," Donovan added, his voice barely audible.

In the long silence that followed, the light in the room shifted. In the distance, thunder rumbled.

"And who do you want to be?" asked Blaine softly.

The question was gentle, but its impact was powerful, like a bolt of lightning. This past year, he'd been so caught up in who he *didn't* want to be, he hadn't really thought about who he was becoming.

Not until this moment.

"I don't know," he murmured, flashing on the image of them running down the hallway that terminated in a wall. Was that his life? Running toward a dead-end destination? Giving too much weight to the past instead of the future?

They stood in the enter of the room, the only sound the piped-in classical music over an intercom. A dramatic piano crescendo seemed to mock Donovan's state of mind.

"Some of the kids actually *stayed* here on prom night," Blaine said lightly. Too lightly, the way one does when purposefully changing the subject.

She's protecting my truth, he realized. The thought infused warmth into the cold epiphany he'd just experienced. "If I'd gone to school with you, I'd have asked you to the prom months in advance to beat out the other guys."

Did she have any idea what power she wielded in

that sweet look of gratitude? It impaled him, right through the heart.

"With such gentlemanly manners, it's hard to believe you didn't fit into the prom scene."

"I was a bit rougher back then. The kind of guy mothers warned their daughters about. Not because I was a Lothario, but because I was always getting into fights. I had more shiners than clothes."

"You seem to handle that temper better now."

"I'm an expert at counting to ten." He grinned. "Probably for the best I wasn't part of the 'prom scene' anyway. A guy in hand-me-downs with a chip on his shoulder? Not a pretty sight. Instead, I hung outside in the parking lot, watching the festivities through a window."

Blaine blinked. "You actually went to the prom, but stayed outside?"

"I had a serious crush on the prom queen, the most popular girl in school. Seems ridiculous in retrospect, but I pined for her like some kind of vengeful Heathcliff."

"Heathcliff," Blaine murmured, nodding. "It fits."

He did a mock double take. "I'm not *that* moody."

"Yeah, right," she teased, tossing him a wink. "At dances I typically hung out behind the gym, playing cards or smoking cigarettes with the nerdy geeks. But prom night, no way. I stayed home."

"With the geeky guys?"

"Nooo. Even most of them had prom dates, believe it or not."

"And none of them asked you?"

She dug her toe into the rug. "I was so one of the guys, none of them even had a passing thought about asking me." She looked around the room, her gaze landing on a painting of a beautiful woman in a gown standing next to a gallant gentleman. "I never told anyone before, but secretly, I yearned to be Cinderella, all dolled up and asked to dance by the dashing prince. I never breathed a word of this to my dad because I feared he'd hire someone to take me to the prom!" She looked back at Donovan. "I know, I don't look the type to have a fairy-tale fantasy, but believe it or not, tomboys sometimes do."

"I believe it," Donovan murmured, thinking how being around Blaine was causing him to almost believe in other things as well. Like pursuing a dream...or falling in love.

A trilling violin solo snagged his attention. The tempo was easy, light.

He held out his hand. "May I have this dance?"

A rose tint stained her cheeks. She hesitated, then slipped her hand into his.

Something wrenched loose inside him as he swept her into his arms, holding her close. He nuzzled her hair, inhaling its freshly washed scent. She held herself stiffly, her feet faltering.

He hugged her closer, murmuring into her ear, "One, two, one, two..." At Princeton, he learned how to dance in the arms of his roommate's sister, a young socialite who turned him on to some of the finer things in life.

Little did he know back then that this sweet moment with Blaine would be by far the finest.

Her body relaxed, softened as she fell into step. They pivoted and swayed as one, caught in a pocket of time where only they existed. On the edge of their world, far away, thunder rolled across the heavens.

A searing bolt of yellow-blue light.

Donovan's gaze darted to the window, catching a jagged line of lightning in the distance. Rain tapped against the glass.

He caught his reflection. And for a surreal moment, he swore he saw the ghost of the man he used to be beckoning to him. The youth he was before learning the depth of his father's deceit. The Donovan who took life, and himself, easier. Who knew how to recognize, and savor, life's sweeter gifts....

It faded, replaced by the image of him and Blaine molded together, swaying to the music. As though his past stepped back to show him his future. A man in love, holding the woman of his dreams, sharing a future.

He tore his gaze from the window and crushed Blaine against his chest, blinking back a sudden surge of emotion. He'd wondered who he would be?

The answer to his future, to the man he wanted to be, was in his arms.

"HELLO, SWEETHEART!" Blaine's dad waved as she slid out of Donovan's pickup.

Donovan caught her as her feet touched the sidewalk.

Her body yielded to him, soft and complying just as it had been when they'd slow danced back at The Broadmoor. The rain fell in inconsistent drops, playing coy again.

Blaine glanced at her dad over Donovan's bulky shoulder. "Hi," she answered, feeling a bit shy at the glow of pride she saw on her father's face. *He's glowing over my "date."*

Donovan shut the passenger door, raised Blaine's hand and pressed a kiss into her palm.

And for a glorious moment, Blaine felt like Cinderella after the ball with the prince escorting her home.

"Don't forget to call Ralph," Donovan whispered.

She nodded. They'd discussed their next strategy to find the bed. She'd continue calling Ralph, Donovan would continue checking eBay. Although she hadn't discussed it with Donovan, Blaine was also ready to place an ad with the local paper, The Gazette.

Donovan turned. "Hello, sir," he said to her father.

"Hello, son."

Son? Blaine's insides quivered. It sounded warm and friendly...and too damn close to matchmaker talk.

"Thanks, Donovan, for lunch," Blaine said quickly, wanting to scamper into work before her father said anything that sounded remotely like "engagement" or "marriage."

"You're welcome," Donovan said warmly.

Blaine looked at him, her heart growing still when she caught that glimmer in his whiskey brown eyes. They'd behaved back at the hotel, sharing a slow dance that lasted several songs, a tender kiss, then hand in hand, they'd left the room.

Mouthing a second thank-you, which she knew Donovan would understand was for letting her fulfill her "prom" dream, she headed for the Blaine Saunders Temporary Agency front door.

"Son," her father said, lagging behind.

Blaine stopped and turned. "Dad—"

"If you don't have plans Saturday evening," her father continued, "I'd like to invite you to my daughter's wedding." He smiled. "My daughter *Sonja's* wedding, I should say, although I'd love to see my other daughter married, too."

Panic flooded her. "Dad! It's time for us to get to work."

"I'd love to, sir, but unfortunately I've made other plans for Saturday night."

"You have?" Blaine blurted.

"Another woman?" her father asked.

In the awkward silence that followed, Blaine was vaguely aware of the growl of thunder in the atmosphere. These past few days, the afternoon storms swirled on the periphery of her life, never hitting full force. What she would give right now for a massive onslaught of rain! It'd get her father inside *fast*.

"No, no," Donovan said.

Did she detect a nervousness in his voice?

Was there another woman?

"I'm driving my mother to her sister's for a bridge game," he continued. "My aunt lives in Parker, and I'd prefer my mother not drive alone."

Blaine nodded rapidly, wishing her father hadn't created a situation where Donovan had to explain not only *what* he was doing, but *why*. Oh, hell, she hadn't helped with her reaction, either. Together, she and her father had forced Donovan to explain there wasn't "another woman."

If only the sidewalk would open up and swallow Blaine whole. Her face hot with embarrassment, she headed inside her business.

A minute later, she heard the front door open and shut, followed by her father's heavy footsteps.

"I can't believe you asked him to the wedding!" Blaine stood at her desk, fidgeting with the miniature NASCAR model. Turning, she paced across the office floor, needing to burn off her agitation.

"I wanted you to have a date," her father said, looking sheepish.

"Dad, I know you want me to marry, but please, *please* don't scare off the one guy who's..." *Who's everything I ever wanted*, she thought with surprise.

She'd felt it last night at the motel, even more at The Broadmoor when Donovan had held her in his arms and cradled her in those slow dances. If a woman didn't watch herself, she'd start thinking the guy was letting down his guard, letting her into his heart.

But even if he was, it was temporary. He'd said as much in different ways. But even if he'd never said a word, one look at his lifestyle spelled out that he didn't want a partner in life. Do Not Enter, Blaine reminded herself.

She set the car back on her desk. Maybe it wasn't too late for damage control. "Just promise me you won't say anything else about Sonja's wedding, or me getting married, to Donovan, okay?"

Her father's apologetic expression lightened. "You'll be seeing him again?"

He was incorrigible. "Maybe."

"Good." Her father looked immensely pleased with himself. "Oh!" he suddenly exclaimed with a start. "I almost forgot! The bank called." He crossed to Blaine's desk and grabbed a blue sticky note. "Wrote the loan manager's name and phone number here."

Blaine's hands turned clammy. She rubbed them against her jeans as she crossed behind her desk. "Oh

Dad, cross your fingers again!" Picking up the phone, she punched in the number scribbled on the sticky note.

Five minutes later, she hung up, her insides plummeting faster than a rock tossed off the summit of Pikes Peak.

"What's wrong?" her father asked, nervously munching a carrot stick. "You were speaking so quietly, I barely heard anything."

She smiled. Now of all times, she wouldn't chide her dad for going for a piece of cake or a candy bar. "They said yes—"

"Hooray!" Her father twirled the carrot stick in the air.

"If I have someone co-sign," she added.

Her father's arms dropped. "Co-sign?"

She nodded.

"Oh, sweetheart." Her father's face sagged. "I'd do it in a heartbeat—"

"Dad, you and I both know the bank wouldn't accept your signature. You live on a meager retirement income. Even if they did let you sign, *I* wouldn't allow it. I don't want you being liable for the loan." She sighed heavily. "And Sonja's out of the question. She works part-time. Plus she and Rudy are going to be counting their pennies for the next few years."

Her father sat quietly, staring so sadly at Blaine, she thought she'd cry if she met his gaze, so instead she stared at the picture of the family, wishing life were as simple and sweet as they made it look with their happy smiles forever frozen in time.

"There's Henry," her father offered.

"He's retired, too, Dad. Plus, how many IOUs can I foist on the guy? No, I can't do that."

Then she thought of who, maybe, could help. It was her only hope.

BLAINE KNOCKED ON THE door, staring at the metallic "4" hung crookedly. She flashed on the day before yesterday when she'd knocked at this same door, desperate to get her bed.

This time, she was desperate to salvage her business.

After a moment, the door opened.

Donovan stood there, his tan face breaking into a lopsided grin when he saw Blaine. "I think your dad should start a dating service," he teased.

In the background, a guitar wailed, accompanied by a sultry saxophone.

"I'm so sorry," Blaine said on a rush of breath. "And I'm embarrassed that I chimed in, wanting to know your plans on Saturday night."

"Are you satisfied there's no other women, besides my mother, in my life?"

Blaine paused, then nodded.

"Then get in here." Donovan scooped her into his arms and swung her over the threshold.

It felt so good, so safe, to be in his embrace again. She held on, savoring his masculine scent, the strength in his body. And when he kissed her, she was glad he was holding her because her body went limp with desire and need.

"I'd carry you to my bed, but I don't have one," he whispered into her ear, his warm breath teasing a sensitive spot behind her lobe.

"I'm sorry for that, too," she murmured.

"You're just one sorry little lady, it seems. What's up?"

He set her on her feet. She wobbled, holding on until the surge of lust subsided. She started to speak, but the words lodged in her throat.

"Did you call Ralph?" Donovan asked, squinting at her curiously.

"No time," she answered, finding her voice. Put yourself first, she reminded herself. *Ask for what you need.* She rolled back her shoulders. "I need a favor."

"Another invitation to Sonja's wedding?" He winked playfully.

"No," Blaine said. She closed her eyes, then opened them. "This is hard for me, but I have no one else I can turn to."

"Do you want to sit down?" He gestured toward the recliner.

"No." She clasped her hands together, mainly to stop their trembling. "A few weeks ago, I filled out an application for a small business loan from the bank."

Donovan stared at her, his eyes growing darker. "I'm listening."

"Well, they called."

He quirked an eyebrow. "And?"

"And...they want someone to co-sign on the loan." Her mouth felt drier than after she'd done that hideous trek to the motel and her throat felt more dirt-caked than her jeans had. "This is hard for me, but you taught me to put myself first, ask for what I need." She sucked in a breath. "I need you to co-sign," she blurted. "I mean..." She struggled to keep her voice level. "...would you please co-sign?"

The following silence was broken by the rattling of the windows accompanied by the splatter of rain.

"Blaine," Donovan finally said, his voice deep, low. "I—"

Lightning crackled, followed by the roar of thunder.

Donovan ached at the look of panic and anguish on Blaine's face. She was putting herself first, yes, but she'd hit him broadside. It was as though all the air had left his body, and he was reeling, grappling for the answer.

He turned and paced a few steps, ending up in front of his bookcase. His gaze landed on the pocketknife.

It was as though it invisibly sliced through him, down to his soul and its secret. "Blaine," he said quietly, not turning around. "My convalescence, when I was fourteen, was because my horse fell on me. Crushed my femur. The shattered bone, and other medical complications, made it a long year."

Blaine murmured a response, indicating she was listening.

"Those months, while I was alone in my room, I accidentally overheard my parents arguing. Over money." He stared at the pocketknife, almost hearing his father's hard, cutting tone. "They were in debt. Again. For as long as I could recall, something was desperately wrong in the family. And then, at fourteen, I discovered my father had betrayed us with his money schemes. Betrayed us by loving the almighty dollar more than he loved his own flesh and blood."

Lightning sizzled and hissed, reminding him of the ever present static that permeated everything in his home growing up.

"I don't think my brothers knew the truth—or if they

did, they never spoke up. My mother obviously knew, but didn't speak up because she didn't want to disrupt the family more than it already was. And my father didn't speak up because his life was a lie."

Donovan picked up the pocketknife. "And after I heard their argument, and realized the truth, I didn't speak up because I was a coward."

He squeezed shut his eyes, hating himself all over again.

Donovan turned to Blaine. "I knew the truth, but I remained silent." Regret and fury coursed through him. "And, a year ago, after my father died, my mother called me, terrified, because creditors were hounding her, threatening to take away her home to fulfill my father's debts."

He met Blaine's eyes, those sweet eyes, so big and full of surprise and concern.

"My retribution is to make it up to my mother for those years I was silent. For the years she took odd jobs—cleaning houses, taking in laundry—just to put food on the table. I want to make up for her pawning her wedding ring so the ranch didn't go into foreclosure. That's why I work so hard—to salvage what's left of the ranch for her future."

"This is why your life is so sterile," Blaine whispered.

Donovan nodded, amazed again at her insights into his shattered soul. "Do you have any ideas the number of documents—IOUs, checks, damn bar napkins—on which I've seen my father's signature this past year?"

Blaine shook her head no.

"Too many." Donovan turned the knife in his hands. "I can't risk signing another agreement. God forgive me, Blaine, but I just can't put my life, my mother's life, into a place where I could conceivably accrue more debt."

Blaine nodded solemnly, her eyes glistening with tears. "I understand," she said in a broken voice. "Really, I do. We're both trying to salvage what is rightfully ours."

Pain seared through Donovan as he wondered if he'd ever again see her tender, open self...or if she'd closed herself off from him forevermore. Maybe he'd let down some of his boundaries, but she now was building her own.

She started to turn, then halted. Looking over her shoulder, she glanced down at the pocketknife, then back to Donovan's eyes.

"You view that knife as a symbol of what your father represented and what you never want to be," she murmured. "Maybe, instead, you should use that knife to cut your spirit free from your past. Sever your emotional ties to your guilt and to your anger. Then, Donovan, you'll truly have your retribution because you'll finally be free."

A moment later, the front door shut with a firm click behind her.

Outside, Blaine walked slowly down the stairs and onto the front lawn of Donovan's building. She'd meant it when she told him she understood. How could she not? Their priority was to protect what was theirs. Donovan, his family home. Blaine, her business.

What they'd shared had been a respite from their burdens, a temporary island from their worries.

The world turned a startling blue with a pop of bright light. Simultaneously, thunder tore through the sky with a punishing boom. Finally, the storm that had always hovered in the distance had arrived.

Blaine turned her face to the threatening heavens.

At one time she'd fantasized the impending storm held the answer to her and Donovan. Their needs and passions for each other would, like the arrival of the storm, finally unveil the truth of what they meant to each other.

And she'd imagined that truth would be the recognition of their mutual love.

In reality, the truth was a chasm they could never cross.

12

A TWENTY-SOMETHING GUY wearing a blue suit and a buzz cut stepped up to the microphone. "This next song is from the Top Gun Rockers to Rudy and his bride." He stepped back and strapped on a guitar. After a nod to the band, they started playing "Take My Breath Away."

Blaine, sipping a beer, tapped her green satin, high-heeled foot in time to the music.

"They're not bad," said her dad, sitting next to her at one of the card tables clustered around the dance floor.

"If they ever decide not to be Air Force pilots, they could get a gig at The Keg," Blaine agreed, smiling. Rudy's pals, who sometimes jammed in a band, had offered their services for the wedding reception. On the dance floor, Sonja and Rudy shimmied and danced.

Blaine glanced at her dad. "Mom would have been so proud."

"Of both of you." He placed his hand on Blaine's. "You've been strong, sweetheart. You did the very best you could."

"What's done is done." How many times had Blaine said that these last few days while packing boxes in the office. It was sad closing up her agency, but to be honest, also a relief. No more fretting about office overhead or keeping people employed. No more taking care of everyone else. Finally, Blaine could just take care of herself, put herself first.

She'd been toying with the idea of contracting her services as a technical writer. Or teaching youth sports at the local Y.

"Your IOU was a thoughtful wedding gift," her dad commented, patting her hand.

"I figured Sonja and Rudy could use a week's worth of handiwork around their new home, wherever they'll be stationed." Her father was being discreet by not mentioning the bed. Sonja had been a dear, too, telling Blaine that it wasn't the gift, but the thought that mattered.

Blaine took another sip of beer, nevertheless fighting a surge of disappointment.

Two days ago, Ralph had finally returned her phone calls. Barry, he explained, was a distant relative who'd been passing through town. Ralph had given him a few delivery gigs to help Barry make ends meet. Only after Blaine's third phone message to Ralph, where she explained the bed was not only misdelivered but lost, had Ralph tried to track down Barry. Unfortunately, he'd left town for whereabouts unknown.

Which meant no one knew where Barry *or* the bed were.

Fortunately, Sonja's new in-laws had given the newlyweds a hefty gift certificate to a department store so Sonja and Rudy had ample money to buy a bed and much more for their new home.

Blaine took another sip of beer. She felt sad about the

whole bed fiasco, but tried not to dwell on it. She had her hands full closing the agency, helping the last few temporary employees wrap up jobs...

And trying every single moment of every day to not think about Donovan.

The last had been more difficult than anything else.

"Another piece of cake?" asked her dad.

"No thanks." She smiled at her dad. "But you go ahead."

"No, I'm on a diet." His gray eyes twinkled. "Besides, two's my limit." He waved at someone across the room. "There's Henry! I'll be right back."

Blaine watched her father walk away, thinking he was not only the greatest dad in the world, but possibly the best receptionist, too. Jerome swore that when his antique business picked up, his priorities were to pay off Ralph, then to hire her dad to help out at the store part-time.

Blaine smiled to herself. *Mom would've been proud of Jerome, too.*

She shifted her gaze to a bank of windows that offered a view of the parking lot. A lone figure stood underneath a light, staring at her.

A couple walked past her table, momentarily blocking Blaine's view. After they passed, she strained to see the figure in the parking lot again. But there was no one. Just a lot filled with cars.

It's been a long week, Blaine thought, fingering her glass of beer. She stared into the liquid, its amber color reminding her of Donovan's eyes.

Images floated through her mind. The two of them

waking up, naked, realizing they were lovers. The night in the Parisian Fantasy room where their desire was hotter than the room's red lights. And then there was the slow dance at The Broadmoor...where, for fifteen minutes, Blaine lived out being the chosen girl at the prom.

"May I have this dance?"

That voice. Husky, deep...

Slowly, Blaine turned her head. "Donovan," she said, her words barely more than a strangled whisper.

His brown eyes glistened as he did a quick appraisal of her. "You look like Cinderella," he murmured.

Her heart hammered foolishly. The sight of that tuxedo, molded to Donovan's buffed body, was almost as electrifying as the first time she saw her gorgeous brass bed.

The man's appeal was devastating.

Her gaze traveled up. Donovan's long hair had been stylishly trimmed, which gave his rugged features a sophisticated edge. And he wore a cologne that smelled like a dangerous mix of testosterone and spice.

"Shall we dance?" he asked again.

She blinked back emotion, wanting more than anything in the world to be with him, to curl into the shelter of his arms, and yet...

So much had changed.

So much had been lost.

"Blaine," Donovan said in a low, husky tone. "It's not just a dance."

And before she could think what he meant by that comment, Donovan had swept her into his arms. Pressing one hand against the small of her back, he pulled her tightly against him and began moving in time to the music.

Blaine pressed her forehead against his throat, praying he didn't feel the trembling in her body. She clung to his jacket with one hand, her other interlaced with his fingers. She closed her eyes, hating the anguish that clenched her heart. He was right, painfully right, to say "it's not just a dance." This closeness was a taste of euphoria that would take her days, months to recover from.

The lights faded. Cool night air washed over her skin. She opened her eyes, realizing Donovan had danced her in the opposite direction of the dance floor.

They stood outside the door that led to the parking lot.

She looked up into his face and met his gaze. "We're losing the music."

"Then let's dance to the tempo of our hearts."

Blaine held back, taking a sobering breath. "Donovan, I can't do this again—"

His fingers pressed lightly against her lips. He dropped his hand to her chin and gently turned her head.

At first she couldn't believe her eyes. Then joy exploded within her. She fought the urge to laugh and cry at the same time.

His pickup was parked at the side of the building. In its back, tied down with ropes, was her magical brass bed.

The moonlight splashed silver on the metal that

curled seductively in the headboard. Each of the four posters, topped with brass knobs, sparkled.

"Where'd you find it?" Blaine stumbled toward the bed, needing to touch it, prove to herself it was real.

"First, I had to find Barry. I'll spare you the details of how I managed *that* miraculous feat. Then I persuaded him to divulge where he dropped off the bed."

Persuaded? Blaine shot Donovan a look. "You didn't—?"

Donovan laughed. "No, that's not my style anymore. Let's just say money doesn't only talk, it also convinces." He caught a look in Blaine's eyes. "It's all right. I've spent a lot of money salvaging the ranch. It's time to salvage something else."

Something else? Don't read more into it. What's done is done. "So," she said, forcing her voice to sound level, together, all the things she didn't feel, "what had Barry done with the bed?"

"He sold it to a used furniture store outside Pueblo."

"And you got it back without the receipt?"

"Barry paid for the bed, then returned it to me. Of course, it helped that I was waiting outside with my pickup." He flashed Blaine a smile that made her ache with longing.

What's done is done.

As night breezes lifted her hair, she shifted her gaze back to the bed. At one time, it symbolized everything she wasn't and everything she secretly desired.

Not anymore.

Since owning this enchanted wonder, she'd experienced white-hot passion and forbidden indulgences.

She'd acted out her fantasies, been desired...been made love to.

Tears gathered in her eyes. "Thank you," she whispered. Donovan would think she was thanking him for finding the bed, but in her heart, she was also thanking him for giving her the gift of her womanliness.

In the background, the band started playing a loud rock-and-roll tune. People were laughing and yelling good-naturedly.

"Do you need to go back to the reception?" asked Donovan.

Blaine thought for a moment. She'd basically spent the day preening over Sonja, from helping her get dressed to holding her train as she walked down the aisle. The only maid-of-honor "duty" Blaine had avoided was catching the bridal bouquet, which disappointed Sonja, but thrilled the teenage girl who snagged it.

"No, I don't need to go back."

"Good." Donovan took her hand. "Let's go for a ride."

AN HOUR LATER, Donovan parked off a back road to the Garden of the Gods, the ancient sandstone rock formations that were preserved as a national monument. After he cut the engine and headlights, they were enveloped in darkness except for the stars above and the floodlights below that cast a golden glow on a section of the rocks commonly called the Kissing Camels.

"Why are we here?" Blaine asked. She'd remained quiet the entire drive out here. She'd been too nervous to talk. It was thrilling to have her bed back, but sheer agony to not know what was going on between her and Donovan.

"It's a beautiful, limitless view," he answered. "A national treasure."

"Are we here to discuss historical monuments?"

"No."

"Then, as you would say," Blaine murmured, "*And?*"

"And...I'm sorry for not co-signing on your loan." The front seat creaked softly as Donovan shifted his weight. "I'm truly sorry, Blaine, it's just that I couldn't—"

"We already discussed this." She didn't want to go there again, to dredge up all the reasons why he couldn't have co-signed. "I understood when you explained the reasons before. There's no reason for us to drive out here and talk about it further—"

"And," he interrupted gently, "I'd like to ask you to manage my consulting business."

She paused. "Manage?"

"Do all the things you're expert at—dealing with corporations, negotiating contracts, balancing the books...and me."

"That last part would be the toughest." She paused. "But I don't want a pity job."

Donovan chuckled. "Never met someone who'd refuse a job because there might be *pity* attached." He gave his head a shake. "First of all, I don't pity you. I admire you. Second, you ran a successful contracting business, which means you have top-notch management expertise. Third, your dad told me all about your skills—"

"My dad?"

"Yes, we had lunch."

She puffed out an exasperated breath. "And when did this happen?"

"I called to see how you were doing, and he asked me to lunch."

"To pitch me as wifey material—"

"Actually, he didn't say the *w* word once. Instead, he told me all about your accounting classes, how expertly you negotiated contracts, stuff like that. That's when I started thinking how great you'd be managing my business."

He waited for Blaine to interrupt. When she didn't he continued, "*And* managing others' consulting gigs. I have some college pals who could also use your business expertise. Like I said, it's everything you already do, minus the office. But you wouldn't need the latter because you could do this from your home. Besides, sometimes you might need to travel." He paused. "For example, I have a pending contract in Alaska."

Alaska. The land she'd always yearned to explore. Exhilaration rippled through her. "It sounds good," she whispered, struggling to keep her wits about her. "Damn good."

"Have you taken your allergy medicine?" he asked.

She arched an eyebrow at him. *Now* what was he up to? "Yes, why?"

He didn't answer. Instead he exited the driver's side and rounded the front of the pickup to the passenger door. When he pulled it open, fresh mountain air wafted in, scented with pine and juniper.

Before she could ask him again what he was doing, he gripped her around the waist and pulled her toward him. "Don't want you to mess up those pretty satin shoes," he explained, lifting her into his arms.

"What about your fancy leather ones?" she countered. A passing breeze blew a tendril of hair across her eyes. She pulled it away with trembling fingers, wishing he'd put her down while also praying desperately he'd never let her go. "Neither of us is dressed for a midnight hike."

"Oh," Donovan said, shutting her door with one foot, "we're not hiking far."

"What about your leg?"

"What about it?"

"I've seen you rub it. It hurts you."

"Only when I've worn myself down. Tonight, I'm rejuvenated."

He carried her to the back of the pickup and set her gently on the ground. He lowered the tail of the truck then bent over, lacing his fingers like a stirrup.

"Step up," he ordered gently.

"But..." She hesitated.

He straightened. "Is there a problem?"

"Well, the bed's in the back of the truck."

"And?"

"And, well, I have nowhere to go but onto the bed."

"As I said, is there a problem?"

Her voice betrayed her emotion. "I can't..."

"Be a legendary lover?" he finished for her. "Because now that we know the legend, we need to make love again on this bed to seal our destiny."

She was so close to Donovan, she swore she could feel his heat. Her body hungered to be with him, but her heart couldn't go there again. "I can't be temporary, Donovan."

There. She said it.

She turned, ready to walk back to the front seat. Ready to go back to picking up the pieces of her life. *What's done is done.*

She'd barely taken a step when strong hands pulled her back. She looked up into Donovan's unyielding profile, outlined in silver from the moon's glow.

"I love you, Blaine," he said gruffly. His fingers feathered her hair, traced her face. "God, yes, I love you. Love how your green eyes sparkle like the sea, revealing the depths of your emotions. I love your sweet smile that makes me believe in life again. Believe in people again. I love your courage...even your bullheadedness." His voice dropped to a husky whisper. "I love how your body feels naked against mine. How you make love with a wild and pure passion that rocks my world."

He gathered her closer, his lips brushing against hers as he spoke. "I'll love you with my dying breath, Blaine, and beyond if God will let me. If I ever prayed for retribution, that would be it. To earn forevermore with you. If that's not permanent, I don't know what is."

"Oh, yes," she murmured, sinking into the velvety warmth of a kiss.

A moment later, he pulled back. In the moonlight she saw the pleased grin on his handsome face. Leaning over, he again laced his fingers.

"Step up, my lady love," he ordered gently. "It's time to claim our place in the ranks of legendary lovers."

She raised her foot. "Napoleon and Josephine."

"Elizabeth Taylor and Richard Burton."

And as he lifted her, she peered through a mist of joyful tears at the sea of stars overhead.

"Donovan and Blaine," she whispered to the sky, imagining her words traveling through the heavens until the end of time.

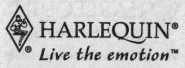

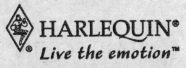

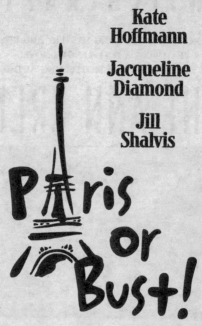

If you enjoyed what you just read,
then we've got an offer you can't resist!

Take 2 bestselling
love stories FREE!
Plus get a FREE surprise gift!

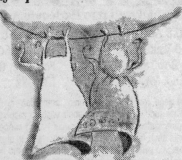
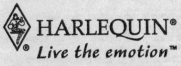